When You Love Somebody

LatimaNicole.com

LatimaNicole

A LatimaNicole Inc. Publishing Company

Copyright © 2015

By LatimaNicole.

New York, NY

ISBN 978-0-692-50280-8

When You Love Somebody

Thank You

I first have to give honor to God who
thought me worthy of ministering to his
children with the gift of words. All praises
are due unto my Father and his Son Jesus
Christ.

My loving parents Willie and Alberta
Williams, who first taught me what it means
to love somebody unconditionally and
unselfishly. I miss you mommy and daddy.

My siblings, Lawrence (AKA Universal)
and his wife Leslie, Kenyetta and her
husband Terry, Malik, Kenti and his wife
Felicia and my brothers from another mother
Love and Born Understanding, thank you
for supporting me, lifting me up and always
keeping me on track. I love you guys with
all of my being.

To my Aunt Diane, you are the matriarch of
our family and I thank you for being a

LatimaNicole

prayer warrior and story teller and for passing down our family's stories for the next generations.

My cousins who were more like brothers and sisters growing up. The Williams' the Gantt girls, The Albert family, The Pearson family, The Grant family, The Brown family, The Bradford family, Robertson family, the Harper family and The Capers/Baker family
Tyrone, Cherie (RIP) Denniel, Paul, Shakeema, Albert Jr., Van, Michelle, Bamidele, Shaimond, Rosie, Roshanna, Nephfetia, Tinaja and Justin and all of my extended cousins I love you to the moon and back.

My sisters, my sisters, my sisters. Do not believe that women do not support each other. I have some amazing women in my life that have become a part of my family. Dineca Robertson, my left hip, Sandra Campbell, my right hip, Tracey Williams

When You Love Somebody

my counselor and advisor, Diane Dennis and Michelle Bradford it doesn't matter how long we go without seeing or speaking to each other, whenever we get together we never miss a step - my forever sisters. Rocky, you are in a class all by yourself and I wouldn't have it any other way. My Gladiators, the love and support that you guys have shown me is priceless. I look forward to us sitting on the beach sipping Gladiator juice © for many years to come.

Fila Antwine, Grei Booker and Jamilah Barnes, thank you for your insight, knowledge and support. My Fly Ladies, Zamara and Natasha EZEE ACCESS TV will be a household name. Mark my words.

Last but not least, I am who I am because of you. I am so thankful that God chose me to bring you into this world. You are my inspiration, my motivation and my greatest achievement. Hakim you have been a blessing to me and anyone you have come in

LatimaNicole

contact with. I know sometimes you may get weary in well doing but heavy is the head the wears the crown my King. I love you from the core of my being.

When You Love Somebody

Prologue

Cami got out of bed and walked over to the French doors that led out to the balcony of her hotel suite. Bourbon Street was packed with people who either wanted to get an early start or hadn't yet made it home. Most of the people who came to New Orleans for the Essence Music Festival never made it to any of the empowerment seminars or workshops. For them it was all parties and bullshit.

The clouds that were forming in the sky were reflective of Cami's mood. Out of the thousands of people that came to the superdome for the nightly concerts, what were the odds that she would run into Matt? She hadn't seen or spoken to him since Keisha and Paul renewed their wedding vows. What a fiasco that was. Cami thought that she had buried her feelings for Matt somewhere deep inside the unreachable corners of her heart. Seeing him yesterday forced all of the emotions she had tried so hard to suppress right back to the surface. As she looked out over the balcony she felt the cool rain drops tickle the back of her neck as she stood contemplating her situation. The crackle of thunder startled her back to reality and she decided to go back inside the room. Someone was knocking at her door. As she padded across the room in her bare feet she wondered who it could be. She knew for sure Keisha wasn't up this early and anyone else would have called the room. As soon as she opened the door, Matt grabbed her in his arms and held her.

"I miss you so much Cami."

"Matt what are you doing here? How did you know where I was staying?"

"It wasn't hard to figure out. I knew you would be staying somewhere close to the action so that you could take some pictures. I just narrowed it down to the better hotels along Bourbon Street."

The look of disbelief she gave him forced him to come clean.

When You Love Somebody

"Okay okay, Keisha told me where you were staying but I promised not to say anything so you can't go cursing her out. Can I come in? We need to talk."

"Matt there is nothing to talk about."

"Cami please!"

As soon as Cami let Matt in, the sky opened up and unleashed a barrage of rain that assaulted the revelers down below who were either to oblivious to it or refused to let the rain dampen their festivities.

Cami picked up her camera and walked out onto the balcony. The rain was unforgiving. It soaked everything in its path. She got a shot of a guy throwing up and thought to herself that the image was the perfect metaphor for her state of mind. She needed to purge Matt from her mind, body and soul and let the rain wash him away.

Matt walked out onto the balcony behind Cami "You have to know that I never meant to hurt you. I want you in my life more than I've ever wanted anything. "

LatimaNicole

He turned Cami around and stared into her eyes.

"All I know is I love you Cami. I would do anything you need me to do. You want me to beg, I'll beg. You want me to stand on this balcony and tell all of Bourbon Street that I'm in love with you I will do it please don't shut me down."

He grabbed her and hugged her for dear life all the while whispering "I love you" in her ear.

"I love you too but…"

Matt put his index finger over Cami's lips and said "no buts." He then led her to the bed where he started to undress her.

"Cami let me make love to you please." Cami knew that she couldn't resist even if she tried so she surrendered.

Matt made love to Cami as if each stroke was a plea to let him back in. Every time he entered her, he did so with such tenderness and longing that it drove Cami to have the most violent orgasm she had ever experienced. As she reached the peak of

When You Love Somebody

desire, it seemed as if the thunder and lightning were an accompaniment to the music she and Matt were making. As her vaginal muscles expanded and contracted and she writhed with pleasure, Cami felt a calmness come over her. In the same instance, in true New Orleans fashion, the rain stopped and the sun began to shine as if nothing ever occurred. And, as Matt lay next to her stroking her hair, she turned her back to him and watched the rain begin to fall again. So many things were running through her mind and she did the only thing that felt right at the moment. Cami cried.

LatimaNicole

Chapter 1
Camille

Cami met Matthew at her cousin Keisha's birthday party. He and Paul, Keisha's husband, grew up together and had been friends since the first grade. They exchanged greetings and Keisha said, 'Matt this is Cami. Cami, Matt was telling me that he wanted to have his kids' picture taken as a gift for his grandparents. They are celebrating their 65th anniversary." She knew Keisha had lost her damn mind if she was trying to do some matchmaking shit. Did she say kids, Cami thought.

"65 years? That's a beautiful thing." she said to Matt. "If and when I get married I hope the Lord blesses me with a marriage that lasts that long."

"Tell me about it." He said. "They are definitely an inspiration to me."

He grabbed her hand and said. "It was nice meeting you Cami. Do you have a business

When You Love Somebody

card so I can call you and set something
up?"

"Sure."

She give him one of her cards. He raised an
eyebrow and said, "I will definitely be
giving you a call. Their anniversary is on
Thanksgiving this year so we don't have a
lot of time."

"OK then. You can reach me at my studio
between 12 and 5 any day except Sunday."

"No doubt. Ladies it's been a pleasure.
Keish, again happy birthday."

Keisha gave him a hug and said, "Matt
you're leaving already? You just got here!"

"Yeah, my aunt is watching the kids for me
and I gotta pick them up. We have an early
day tomorrow."

Keisha poked out her bottom lip and said,
"Okay hon give my babies a kiss for me."

Cami had to admit the boy had swagger. He
was definitely the type of dude she would be
attracted to. He had to be at least 6'2", with
broad shoulders, skin the color of warm
caramel and he was clean cut. None of that

pants sagging, dirty cornrows, thug shit. He looked damn sexy in his brown corduroy blazer, orange sweater vest, and brown Gucci loafers. Not to mention his cologne smelled so good she could feel a fire growing in her groin just from getting a whiff of it. She turned to Keisha and said, "Keisha it's good to see a brother handling his business. It must be hard being a single dad."

Keisha rolled her eyes and said, "Shit he might as well be a single father with that trifling wife of his. I can't stand that heifer."

"Oh his wife was here?"

"Hell no! She knows I don't like her stinking ass, she wouldn't dare come to my party."

"Oh I just assumed since he said something about picking up the kids."

"Please knowing that chick she probably cut out before he did so she wouldn't have to stay home with the kids. I never saw no shit like it before. Matt runs around like Mrs.

When You Love Somebody

Doubtfire. He does everything. He cooks,
cleans, does homework, hair, laundry,
shopping and still finds time to be in the
studio making hits. All that broad does is
party and spend money."

"Wow. That's crazy. She got it good. You
can barely get the average dude to pay child
support let alone anything extra."

"That's why I can't stand her. She got a
good man and don't even appreciate him."

"You know it's always like that. If the man
is good, the woman is trifling, if there is a
good woman at home, the man is a dog."

"You know I think divorce shouldn't be an
option, but I told Matt he needs to kick her
ass to the curb."

"Speaking of trifling, where's your other
half?"

"Let's not go there. You know he's slow as
all hell. He just called and said he's on his
way."

"How is everything with you two? Is Paul
still acting like the world's oldest teenager?"

"You know it. But I can't stress myself over him and I don't want to talk about it anymore. It's my birthday and I'm not going to let anyone ruin it for me. So let's get a drink and hit the dance floor. I told the DJ to play some old school hip-hop. I'm ready to get my groove on. You know how we used to tear it up at the jams in Ajax Park."

"Yeah okay disco duck don't be calling me in the morning talking about your knees hurt. You're 35 not 25."

"Whatever heifer, come on."

Chapter 2
Matthew

The first thing Matt noticed about Cami was her titties. When Keisha introduced them he couldn't help but notice her headlights shining, beaming through the fabric of her Dolce and Gabanna T-shirt. He had to tell myself not to be obvious but her

When You Love Somebody

rock hard nipples turned him the fuck on.
Keisha snapped him back to reality by
reminding him about the pictures; but now
all he could think about was sucking on
Cami's breast and burying his face in her
cleavage. Damn, He had never met a
woman he was this attracted to. Before he
got married, he had his fair share of women
but his relationships were more business
than personal. He always had a couple of
chicks that he dealt with at any given time
and they all served a purpose. He made sure
that he surrounded himself with ride or die
chicks that would do whatever he needed
them to. He had one chick that he fucked
with because she had good credit and owned
her own crib; she leased all his cars for him.
Another chick let him use her crib to stash
his drugs and whenever he needed her to
make a drop off or pick up she was down for
it. Louise was his little shortie and he used
her crib for cooking, cutting and bagging his
crack. For Matt it was never about looks, it
was about money. But he left all that behind

him when Louise got pregnant. He had to leave that street shit alone because he didn't want to be like his Pops and spend the first years of his seed's life locked down. He was never in love with Louise but she was the mother of his children and he always promised himself that if he ever had kids he would make sure they had the family life he missed growing up. If that meant staying married for their sake so be it. He was prepared to make that sacrifice. But Cami made him question if he was making the right choice. She was everything he wanted in a woman. When he thought about her he feel good inside and she made him smile. Cami was the type of woman who was unaware of her sexuality. He could tell she never tried to be sexy. She just was. The more he thought about her the more the realization set in that He wanted to see her again. He needed to see her.

When You Love Somebody

Chapter 3

Camille

"Reflections, Camille speaking."

"Hello. Hello."

Cami knew there better had not been anyone playing around on the phone.

"Hi Camille, its Matt."

"Who?"

"Matthew. We met at Keisha's birthday party."

"Yes. Mr. Gucci loafers."

"That be me. So I see you were checking me out."

"Not really. I just appreciate a brother with some style."

"Ouch that hurt. But anyway, I apologize for not speaking up when you answered the phone, but you threw me off with your voice."

"What do you mean by that?"

LatimaNicole

Nothing. Never mind. I'm calling to set up an appointment. When can I bring the kids to your studio?"

"First let me tell you how I work. Since I will be taking pictures of the kids I would like for us to spend some time together so that I can get to know them and also so they can become comfortable with me. This way when we do the shoot I can capture their personalities. I hate doing posed pictures. To me they are so unnatural and stiff. How old are your kids?"

"My son who is the oldest is 10 and my daughters are 6 and 4. By the way I like the idea of spending time with them. But I must warn you, they can be a lot to handle at times."

"Will you be in the pictures?"

"Nah. Originally I wanted it to be a family portrait but my wife wasn't for it."

"Sorry to hear that."

"Don't be sorry, it is what it is. How's Saturday look for you?"

When You Love Somebody

"This Saturday? I doubt that I'll be available but hold on let me pull up my calendar." Cami pulled up her outlook calendar and told him the bad news.

"It looks like I'm booked until the middle of November."

"Damn. Keisha said you were official but I had no idea. Like I was telling you I'm kind of on a deadline. The party is in eight weeks. Is there anything you can do?"

"Let me see if I can move some things around and I'll get back to you. Give me your number and I'll call you later."

"How about I call you later. I'll be in the studio until about 2:30 and then I have to pick the kids up from school. Will you be available around 3, 3:30?"

"I have a client coming in any minute now and depending on how the shoot goes, I should be. Just call me."

"Okay, talk to you later."

"Alright."

LatimaNicole

That was an interesting conversation, Cami thought. She'd have to remember to press Keisha about that dude.

When You Love Somebody

Chapter 4

Matthew

"Yo Matt this track is bananas." Paul said.

"You feeling it huh? Wait 'til you hear the joint I did for this new artist coming out named Rasheed. The boy is crazy, he reminds me of Maxwell with a Sam Cooke/Otis Redding flavor. Listen to this." Matt cued up the track and Rasheed's voice flooded the studio. He could tell by the way P was leaned back on the couch that the joint was fire.

"That's some real baby making shit right there son. Make me want to go home and beat it up. Keisha been talking that baby shit, she might just get her wish fucking around with you and Rasheed."

"That's what's up. Yo, what's the deal with her girl Cami? I called her to get it poppin with the photo shoot thing. Yo son her voice is crazy on the phone."

LatimaNicole

"Let me find out Mr. Do Right is stepping
over to the bad side. It's about time. But
real talk, I can't tell you much about her cuz
she can't stand me. She caught me with one
of my jump offs in Jamaica, took pictures
and sent them to Keisha. That broad was
out of pocket for that bullshit but that's her
cousin and they tight like gnat booty."
I remember that. I don't know how you got
out of that one man but one of these days
that playa playa shit is gonna catch up to
you."
"Nigga you know me. What my man Jigga
said? Slick like a gato. Keisha ain't going
nowhere, she know how good she got it. As
long as I keep her in Gucci and Louis, buy
her a new whip every couple of years and
pay all the bills, I'm good. But anyway, you
checking for Cami?"
"Nah man, it's just that her voice is ill.
Remember that Spike Lee movie 'Girl 6'?
When home girl answered the phone? That's
my word I thought I called a phone sex
line."

When You Love Somebody

"You crazy. If you was to push up she probably wouldn't give you the time of day especially if she know about Louise. Cami don't play that married shit. Yo you remember L from Sutphin?"

"Yeah I ain't seen that dude in years."

"We kick it from time to time. One time me, him, Keisha and Cami went to this party. He tried to kick it to Cami and made the mistake of keeping it real and telling her he was married. She barked on dude so bad he couldn't even look at her for her the rest of the night. She had him under so much pressure that when we were ready to bounce he took a cab home instead of riding back to Queens with us."

"Speaking of bouncing, I gotta go pick up the kids."

Come on man I wanna finish this track. Why can't Louise pick them up?"

"You know I pick up the kids everyday so fall back."

"I'm telling you man you need to put your foot down. I could see if you was running around in the street crazy, but you busting your ass working and holding it down. That shit is crazy."

"Look man I feel you but my home life is just that MY home life and I don't want to talk about it."

"I respect that. Do what you gotta do and hit me up later."

"Aight son. One."

"Daddy tell Sonny we going to get our pictures took today. He don't believe me."

"Daddy tell Maya we just going to meet the lady we ain't taking no pictures today."

As soon as the kids got in the car they started bickering.

"First of all where did you two learn to speak like that? Maya we are not having our pictures taken today we are just going to meet Ms. Camille. Okay."

"See told you Maya. You think you know everything."

"I know more than you dumb dumb."

"That's enough from the both of you. I want all three of you on your best behavior you

When You Love Somebody

hear me. That means no touching anything, speaking only when you're spoken to and staying in your seats. Do you hear me?"

"Yes Daddy."

"I can't hear you."

"YES DADDY!" They screamed in unison.

"That's better. We're here. Sonny help your sister out of her car seat."

"She sleep."

Okay I'll get her. You and Maya get out on the other side."

"Daddy I hate when you pick us up in the truck."

"Why is that Maya?"

"Cause I can't never get out by myself."

"That's cause you a shrimp."

"Shut up Sonny you always talking about somebody like you a giant."

Matt took Misa out of her car seat and said, "Don't start. I'm telling the both of you right now don't let me embarrass you in there. Maya ring the bell. "

"Okay Daddy."

LatimaNicole

Cami's voice came over the intercom and even with the static he could still hear the sexiness.

"Can I help you?"

"Cami its Matt. I figured I would stop by since your studio is so close to the kids' school. I hope it's okay."

"It's fine come on up."

When You Love Somebody

Chapter 5
Camille

This Negro had nerve, Cami thought. He was lucky everything went smooth with her client. She hoped he wasn't one of those dudes that thought the world revolved around him. She didn't get that vibe but you never knew. When she opened the door Matt was standing there with his three kids looking like a page out of a fashion magazine. The little girl he was holding was dressed in a pink Juicy Couture sweat suit and a pair of pink and white Nike Airmax. The older girl had on a Burberry cardigan and matching skirt with a pair of ballerina flats and the boy, who was the spitting image of his Dad, was wearing a Polo sweater, jeans and a pair of Prada sneakers. Talk about advertising.

"Hello guys please come in. My name is Camille. Matt please introduce me to these beautiful babies."

LatimaNicole

"Thanks Cami. This knucklehead here is Matthew Jr., but we call him Sonny. Miss Missy over here is Maya and sleeping beauty is Misa."

"Nice to meet you all. Please make yourself at home."

The kids began to walk around, but Matt cleared his throat and they made a B line for the couch. He had his kids in check. She liked that. S saw that Matt was struggling with the baby and said,

"Matt you can have a seat."

"Thanks, this girl is heavy. I gotta stop feeding her."

Cami couldn't stop staring at his sexy eyes so she turned her attention to the kids.

"Your Dad told me that you wanted to take a couple of pictures."

Maya spoke up first and Cami could tell she was the outgoing one. Sonny was laid back and quiet like his dad.

"Ms. Camille I want to be a model when I grow up. Can you take some pictures of me

When You Love Somebody

by myself? I want to put them in my scrapbook."

"I don't see why not. How about I take a couple of each of you by yourself? You like that idea?"

Sonny said, "That's cool with me. I need some new pictures for my blog."

Maya put her hand on her hip and said, "That's not fair. Daddy why Sonny get to have a blog and I can't?"

"Maya we'll talk about it later," Matt said then turned to Cami, "So now that you've met the rug rats how can you resist them? I was hoping that the cute kid charm would persuade you to move some things around and fit us in."

"Unfortunately I wasn't able to rearrange my schedule but I tell you what, I don't usually work on Sundays but I'll make an exception for these cutie pies. Is this Sunday good for you? It's supposed to be nice so maybe we can go to the park."

"Sunday sounds good."

"Sunday at 11? I'll bring lunch."

LatimaNicole

"11 is cool but you don't have to do the lunch thing. It will be my treat. It's the least I can do for you helping a brother out."

"Okay then." Cami turned to the kids and put her arms out.

"I'll see you guys on Sunday. Can I have a hug?"

The oldest two gave her a hug but little Misa wasn't having it.

"Bye Ms. Camille."

"See you Sunday guys."

After the photo shoot, as soon as Matt had everyone settled in the car and on their way home, Maya started in on Matt with her questioning.

"Daddy is Ms. Camille your girlfriend?"

"Maya where did you get that from?"

"That's what Sonny said. He said all men have a wife and a girlfriend and you have mommy and Ms. Camille."

Where do kids come up with this shit? Matt said to himself shaking his head.

When You Love Somebody

"No baby girl. Ms. Camille is not my girlfriend. She's your Auntie Keisha's cousin and she's doing us a favor."
He reminded himself to have a talk with that boy find to find out where the hell he was getting that mess from.
"The only woman I have in my life is your mother and that's the way it's supposed to be."
"If Mommy wasn't your wife would Ms. Camille be your girlfriend then?"
"What is this girlfriend business about? Your Mom is the only girl I want okay. End of story."
"Okay but if she was your girlfriend it would be okay because I like her."
He started to realize that he liked her too. When he brought the kids to the studio, he couldn't help but notice how good she looked. She had on a pair of dark blue jeans that showed off her hips. Not to mention they had so much fun today. Cami had him meet her at Fort Totten Park and the kids got to run around and play while Cami snapped

picture after picture. Then they had lunch at Jackson Hole. The kids were bugging out over how big the burgers were. Sonny tried to bet Matt that he could eat all of his burger. The damn thing was bigger than his face. Matt had to stop him so he wouldn't get sick. Then they made their way to Cami's studio where she worked her magic. She even managed to get him to take a couple of flicks. The kids were acting like celebrities on a red carpet. He realized that he had keep a close eye on Maya; she was off the hook for a six-year-old. He had to admit Cami was mad cool. They talked about a lot of things. Of course she tried to get all up in his business but he wasn't having it. She was definitely easy to talk to. He did get to know her a little bit better and truth be told he wouldn't mind seeing her again. He could see himself picking her brain about a few things. It was always nice to get a woman's perspective.

When You Love Somebody

Chapter 6
Camille

Keisha was fuming when Cami got to the restaurant. She was supposed to meet her an hour ago. She couldn't believe she was on the phone with Matt for over two hours. Where the heck did the time go?

Keisha and Paul owned a neo-southern style restaurant on Dekalb Avenue in Fort Greene Brooklyn. They got a nice crowd during the week but on the weekend it was always at least an hour wait for a table. They were known all over the city for their Sunday Jazz brunch. Keisha did her thing in the kitchen, Cami couldn't front. She rushed into the restaurant kissed the hostess on her cheek and saw Keisha walking toward her.

"Hey baby cakes."

"Don't baby cakes me. Where the hell you been?"

LatimaNicole

"I am so sorry. I got caught up with a client who wanted to go over some proofs. She had me take all of these pictures of her ugly ass and then kept saying she didn't like them. I wanted to tell her that all the PhotoShop in the world wasn't gonna help her. She needed Dr. 90210 or that show The Swan.

Okay so she was lying. But that broad had been getting on her nerve so it wasn't a complete lie.

Anyway, she wasn't ready to talk about Matt yet; she didn't want anyone to get the wrong idea.

"Yeah, yeah, tell me anything. You keep me waiting an hour again and I know something. You're lucky this is my restaurant. When you text me to tell me you were on your way I went ahead and ordered for us since you always get the same thing."

"That's right I got my mouth all tuned up for the sweet potato crumble and catfish fingers. So what's been up darling? I haven't seen you in a minute."

When You Love Somebody

"Same soup different bowl. Hubby getting on my nerves as usual, but other than that not much."

"I don't know why you keep putting up with his bullshit. You're too good for his crap. If I was you I would have been packed my bags. But I'm not you and before you say it, I know he's your husband for better or worse, blah, blah, blah."

"Cut it out Cami. Must we do this every time? Please keep my marriage out of the conversation. I'm stressed out enough."

"What happened now?"

"He hasn't been home since last Friday."

"What? Have you spoken to him?"

"Yeah. He calls me every day."

"Where is he?"

"He claims he went to Miami for the Video Music Awards. But I'm not stupid. That shit was on Monday. It's Thursday and his behind still ain't home. I'm getting tired of him Cami."

"So what are you going to do about it?"

LatimaNicole

"What can I do? He's my husband, marriage is supposed to be forever."

"Humph. Not when you're the only one who remembers that they're married. I bet he doesn't even wear his wedding band."

"Chile please. That lasted all of a month, then he claimed it was getting too tight and he needed to get it sized. Needless to say I never saw the thing again."

"Damn shame. But enough about Larry the Loser, girl I need a vacation. We gotta plan something quick cause if I don't get a change of scenery soon I'm gonna blow a gasket."

"Where you wanna go?"

"Somewhere with some white sand and blue water."

"Girl you know its hurricane season I ain't messing with you."

"How about Cali? We could fly out to LA and chill for a couple of days."

"Okay Big Wilma you must be snapping a bunch of flicks these days."

When You Love Somebody

"Please don't hate the player hate the game baby girl. On the real though, you in? If not I don't have a problem going by myself."

"When are you trying to go? I have the restaurant show coming up in like two months."

"Two months? I'm trying to leave in like two weeks."

"That might be a bit too soon but set something up for the end of the month and e-mail me the details. I gotta get back in the kitchen. You know it gets crazy in here."

"I'm on it. Love you baby cakes."

"You don't love me, you just using me for my catfish fingers."

"Whatever heifer, I'll call you later."

Cami left the restaurant and decided to go back to her studio to finish up some work. The telephone was ringing as she walked through the door and she made a dash for it but the caller was gone and all she heard was a dial tone.

As soon as she hung up the phone rang again.

LatimaNicole

"Reflections, this is Camille."

"What's up Cami?"

"How are you Matt?"

"Good. Listen, the kids loved the pictures and they wanted me to invite you to the party."

"I don't know about that Matt."

"I didn't think you would want to come but I had to ask. You're all the kids talk about since they saw the pictures. I let them choose which one we're going to give my grandparents and they chose the one with the four of us at the park with the bridge in the background. Is that crazy or what? All that time we spent in the studio, go figure."

"That's kids for you, you say left and they go right. But anyway tell them I said hi and I'm sorry I can't make it but I'll be in California Thanksgiving weekend."

"Oh, you and your man going to visit the family for the holidays?"

Now this Negro thought he was slick, Cami thought. She never told him she had a man.

When You Love Somebody

He must have been fishing for information.
Just for that she decided to play along.

"We won't be visiting family, just going on vacation."

"Sounds like fun. LA is a cool place to visit; I couldn't live there though. It's too fake for me. I'm from the hood. You know we don't do fake in the hood."

"I hear you but we won't be staying in LA, we're renting a beach house in Malibu."
Cani thought she detected a bit of jealousy in his voice. He had some nerve with his married ass.

"Okay well have a good time and I'll talk to you later."

"Alright then. Peace Matt."
She hung up the phone thinking what the hell was that about? At the same time she was smiling on the inside. What was it about this dude that had her drawn to him? She was glad she didn't have to deal with him anymore, it could get dangerous.

LatimaNicole

Keisha and Cami were on their way to the airport when her phone rang.

"Hello."

"Hi Cami how are you today?"

"I'm good and yourself?"

She was hoping Keisha didn't see the big Kool-Aid smile she had on her face. She hadn't spoken to Matt in about two weeks and she wondered why he was calling her now.

"I know you're on your way to the airport and I just wanted to say have a safe trip."

Oh my goodness he remembered she thought, how sweet.

"Thank you."

"Is something wrong?"

"Not at all."

"So what's with the short answers? Oh my bad, you probably can't talk right now right?"

"Not really."

"No doubt. Again, have a safe trip."

"Thanks for calling."

When You Love Somebody

"Aight. Don't have too much fun and I'll talk to you later."

She hung up the phone and realized she was still smiling and had little butterflies in her stomach. This was not good.

"Who was that and what were they saying that got you cheesing like a little school girl?"

Leave it to Ms. Bonita not to miss a beat.

"That was Matt."

"Matt who? I know you're not talking about Married with three kids Matt?"

"The one and only."

"Okay what the fuck is going on? I know Ms. 'I don't mess with married men' is not messing with a married man."

"Whatever heifer. For your information I am not messing with a married man. You know I don't get down like that but there is something about him that I can't explain. He gives me butterflies."

"Oh my goodness! Somebody finally melted the ice queen! Matt is a good dude caught up in a crazy situation and I love him to death. He holds his family down and with all the drama he goes through with his wife, he's never cheated on her."

"He seems like a good dude. I was so impressed with how he interacted with his kids. Especially his daughters. Keish you should have seen him in the studio doing their hair and fixing their clothes, and the sad part was not once did the kids mention their mother. I am dying to find out what the deal is with them but when I asked him about it he shut me down"

"He's talked to me about certain things but he knows I don't like Louise so he doesn't really confide in me. You know if you think about it Matt and I are in the same boat. When you sent those pictures of Paul in Jamaica, I called Matt but you know that's his boy so he didn't want to get involved."

"I hear that. You know the good OLE boys always stick together."

"Sure do. But I'm not trying to ruin this vacation thinking about Paul and his mess. As soon as we get on this plane I'm going to

When You Love Somebody

get me a drink and get some sleep. Wake me when we land."

Cami wished she could get Matt out of her head but he was all she'd been thinking about since he called.

Slow down Camille, she told herself, you're lusting after somebody else's husband. No matter what their marital situation is, he's still married and you need to respect that. With that she put her eye mask on and prepared to sleep until they landed.

"Hey Cami its Matt. I was wondering if I could come by the studio tonight to look over the proofs from the photo shoot. We need to choose a cover like yesterday. The label pushed up the release date and now we're scrambling to wrap everything up."

"I don't see why not."

"That's what's up. So I'll see you around nine."

"See you then."

"Peace."

Cami struggled to get through the rest of her day without thinking about Matt but to no avail. She had to really make a conscious effort to stay focused. Finally he rang the buzzer and she damn near jumped out of her skin. She buzzed him in and he looked even better than she remembered. Damn it was going to take every ounce of self-control she had not to jump on this man.

"Cami I really appreciate you doing this. I know you must think I do everything at the last minute, but trust me I'm not like that at all. This music business is crazy. It's a lot of hurry up and wait."

"I understand. I've dealt with plenty of artists and industry people before, it helps to be flexible."

Matt came behind her while she was bent over her MAC looking at the proofs, leaned over her and whispered, "Are you?"

"Am I what?"

"Flexible?"

Then he started to nibble on her earlobe.

Her mind was telling her, okay Cami you have to put a stop to this, the man is married.

When You Love Somebody

But her body was screaming, oh, but it feels so good I don't want him to stop.

Mind: He has to stop. Cami you know there's no turning back after this.

Body: Cami shut up and go with the flow you know you want to.

"Matt we can't do this." she said as he left a trail of fire down the side of her neck with his kisses.

"Do what? Am I doing something wrong?"

Body: If this is wrong I don't want to be right.

Mind: But I don't sleep with married men. I don't sleep with married men, I d o n t s l e e p w i t h

m a r r i e d m e n.

Oh my goodness. He pulled her head toward his and started to kiss her. His lips were so thick and soft she could have sucked on them for hours. He pulled her ponytail so that her head jerked back, stuck his tongue in her mouth and performed a search and rescue operation. Matt was making her feel things she hadn't felt in a long time. She was so aroused she could feel her nipples straining against her lace bra.

"Cami I want you so bad, I need you in my life."

Shut up and keep kissing me, her mind screamed. Hot damn! He took her breast out of her shirt and she grabbed the back of his head while he teased her nipple with his tongue. When he put it in his mouth and started to suck on it, she damn near passed out. Cami started to gyrate up against his rock hard penis and he moaned with pleasure.

"Ms., Ms."

What the hell was going on? Whose voice was that, she questioned.

"Ms. I need you to put your seatbelt on please. We're about to land."

Whew it was a dream. Thank goodness she said to herself because she didn't think she could have held out.

Keisha immediately zeroed in on her once she had buckled her seat belt.

When You Love Somebody

"So, Ms. Cami what or who were you dreaming about?"

"I don't know what you're talking about."

"Yeah okay. All that moaning you was doing. Whoever he is he must have been putting it down. Let me find out you had a wet dream on the plane."

Cami's face must have given it away because she looked at her and said, "Ooooh you were dreaming about Matt. I knew it. I knew you were kicking it with him."

"Kicking it? Not hardly. He's a nice guy but that's somebody's husband slash problem and you know I don't get down like that."

"Cami I don't know why you always trying to play tough guy. One of these days you're gonna meet your match and he's going to knock you right off of your feet and there won't be a damn thing you can do about it. I know you always try to analyze shit and play it out in your mind but love doesn't work like that honey. Sometimes you don't get to choose who you fall in love with."

LatimaNicole

"Love? Chill with the L word Keish. Where the fuck did all that come from? How we go from me dreaming on the plane to falling in love?"

"I'm just saying."

"Well stop saying and get your luggage so we can get out of this airport."

"Change the subject if you want to but you know I'm right. Matt might just be the one to rip your heart right out of your chest and it won't be a damn thing you can do about it."

"Whatever heiffer."

"I got your heifer. How are we getting to the hotel? I hope we're not taking no shuttle bus. You know buses make me sick."

"Chill out Keish. We are balling this weekend. We gotta pick up the car over there."

"Over where? I know you don't mean over where it says VIP car rentals."

"Just hush and let me go get the keys."

When You Love Somebody

They walked out to the parking lot, Cami pressed the car alarm and said, "There's our car right there."

Keisha slid her shades down her nose, looked at her and said, "Do you have an inheritance you're not telling me about? Are you selling something besides pictures? Not only would you not allow me to pay for my half of the trip, but you rented a CLK convertible? Start talking Missy."

"Be easy Keisha. No, I'm not balling. You know that is not my style. The car comes with the hotel package and what better way to see Malibu than in a drop top?"

Cami was truly impressed. If the car was any indication of the rest of the vacation package her and Keisha were going to have a ball.

"Keish you want to drive? I want to get some pictures of the scenery."

"Hell yeah I want to drive. Drop the top baby. Californ I A. You got any Tupac in your Ipod?"

"Girl you crazy. Chill for a minute and let's get out of this LA traffic before you start bugging the fuck out"

"True. Traffic over here is the worse."

The traffic actually wasn't that bad which was a good thing because after sitting on a plane for six hours, Cami would have lost it if they had to sit in traffic too. According to the directions, after they jumped on the 405 they would be there in no time.

The scenery was amazing. The Pacific coastline was so tranquil and peaceful. Cami couldn't wait to get to the hotel and hit the beach. They pulled up to the hotel and Keisha started bugging again. You would think she had never been anywhere.

"Oh my goodness Cami this hotel is amazing. Okay are you going to tell me how the fuck you pulled this off? Let me know now because you know I love you like a sister but I ain't going to jail for nobody."

The hotel was beautiful. Cami figured she had better tell the fool she was there on a

When You Love Somebody

freelance assignment before she had a coronary.

"Keisha, I can't lie to you."

"I knew it. I knew it. What kind of bullshit you done got me into?"

"Keisha for real you gonna make me hurt you. You know damn well I'm not into no shady shit. This is a working vacation courtesy of Essence Magazine. I'm writing a review for their annual spa series, so relax and enjoy yourself."

"You didn't tell me you were working for Essence. Hell I didn't even know you started writing."

"Do I have to tell you about every freelance job I get?"

"No, but its Essence Cami, that's a big deal."

"I guess it is. We have been reading Essence ever since we learned how to read, dreaming about being like the women we read about in the articles. Look at us now. My career is taking off; and you own one of

the hottest restaurants in Brooklyn. We
doing our thing girl."

"And you know this man! Remember when
I used to cut out all the recipes and test them
out on you and Kevin?"

"Do I remember? Shit, half the time your
concoctions were the only thing I had to eat.
Enough of the reminiscing, grab that Gucci
luggage and let's do the damn thing."

They got to the room and it was amazing.
The suite turned out to be a beachfront
cabana with French doors that led onto a
patio and had direct access to the beach.
Cami immediately picked up the phone to
make their spa appointments while Keisha
took a tour of the suite.

"Keisha, I'm on the phone with the spa
attendant, what services do you want to
get?"

"I didn't look at the brochure yet. I can't get
over this patio. The view is so peaceful.
Thank you."

"Girl please, we're sister cousins. We might
not always see eye to eye but you know I got

When You Love Somebody

your back. Now enough of that mushy shit, what services do you want?"

"What are you getting?"

"The 'Chai Soy Mud Wrap'; the brochure says,

This treatment begins with a Papaya Pineapple Grape seed scrub. Papaya helps soften the skin and is very beneficial to dry sun-damaged skin. Pineapple is an excellent anti-inflammatory and grape seed is a powerful anti-oxidant. The rich nutrients of Epicurean's Chai Soy Mud will then be applied. You will be wrapped to activate the mud's healing properties. This helps to draw out toxins from soft tissue layers while smoothing and tightening your skin. Epicurean's Papaya Pineapple lotion with anti-aging enzymes will be applied at the conclusion of the treatment.

"Then I'm getting a deep tissue massage."

"Book me for the same thing; I need to detox. Those damn cigarettes are making my skin look old as hell."

"So why don't you stop smoking Einstein?"

"Shut up. What time is our appointment? Do
I have time for a nap?"

Yeah, actually we have like two and half-
hours. I'm going to take a walk on the
beach and take a couple of pictures. I'll
meet you back here."

"Okay."

"Hello."

"Hi Matt its Cami."

"Hey Ma what up? How was your flight?"

"It was good I just wanted to call and let you
know I got here safe."

"I'm happy to hear that but truthfully; I
really don't want to think about you and
your man's vacation."

"Matt, I'm here with Keisha."

"Oh word. When you said you couldn't talk
I automatically assumed."

"Yeah and you know what happens when
you assume. You make an ass out of
yourself"

"Touché'."

Cami thought she detected a smile in his
voice.

When You Love Somebody

"Let me find out you on the other end of the phone cheesing. Question, why does it matter to you if I'm here with my man or not?"

"Cami, on the real it shouldn't but I'm gonna keep it funky; I was real tight when I got off the phone with you earlier."

"But why?"

"I think you know why."

"No I don't that's why I'm asking."

"You want me to put it out there? Okay fuck it. I like you Cami. I can't explain it but I know I like your style. You got your shit together and that's so attractive to me."

"Is that right?"

"Not to sound conceited or anything but I know you feeling me too."

"Since you know so much; tell me why if I have my shit together like you say, would I be checking for a married man?"

"I didn't say you were checking for me. Are you?"

"No, I'm not. Don't get me wrong, if we were in another place or time I would be. I definitely like the way you move and how you are there for your kids, but again you're married."

"Cami, you don't have to keep reminding me. Trust me I know I'm married and I have never cheated on my wife. But somehow you got under my skin. I've been thinking about you a lot since the photo shoot and if nothing else I would like for us to be friends."

Was he fucking serious, her brain screamed, "Friends?" She couldn't be his friend when all she could think about was shoving her tongue down his throat.

"Friends it is."

"That's what's up. So what's on your agenda for today?"

"Me and Keish have a spa session in a couple of hours and after that we'll probably hit the streets. We got a drop top CLK with the package and I plan on putting that joint to good use."

"I hear that hot shit. You behave yourself out there. Don't let me and my boy P have

When You Love Somebody

to take the red eye out there and tear some shit up."

"Please, your boy P probably glad Keisha's out here so he can be in the street doing his thing."

"Okay, next subject."

"Why are ya'll even friends? You seem to be exact opposites. Unless you frontin for me."

"Nah babe I don't have to front. What you see is what you get. But on the real me and P been down since the first grade. I know if nobody else got my back P do and vice versa. The shit we did coming up in this industry alone was bananas not to mention when we was out there scrambling in the hood. I just got my shit together once I had my son."

"I don't know why Keisha put up what his shit. Don't get me wrong, P a good dude but he's a fucked up husband, just straight disrespectful. Shit he act like Keisha need him for something. He forgets when his ass was trying to get on who was taking care of

LatimaNicole

him, paying for studio sessions with her student loan money. Niggas kill me."
Breathe Cami.
"You don't have to tell me. I was there I know. He can't front on Keish. Shit she even held me down when I was fucked up."
"I don't know why I never met you before now if you been around that long."
"Probably cause I was on some next shit back then. Music money and broads. I'm telling you Ma I was ruthless back then. If you would have met me like ten, eleven years ago you'd be saying the same thing about me."
"So what made you straighten up and fly right?"
"My son. I wanted him to have the family I didn't have when I was growing up. My childhood was fucked up. The only thing my Pops ever gave me was his name. He used to come around when he felt like it and my Moms was getting high so I basically had to fend for myself. If it wasn't for my grandparents, I probably woulda been in the

When You Love Somebody

system for real. You know how crazy South Side was back then. Niggas getting money and getting caught up. My Pops was one of them get money old school dudes you know running numbers, slinging heron and when that crack shit hit he started getting high and turned my Moms out. Shit was crazy. After old dude got locked up Moms just fell the fuck off."

"I'm sorry you had to go through that but on the flip side that struggle made you the man you are today."

"Damn Cami, what the fuck? I'm telling you shit I never told nobody. Not even my wife. It's bananas how comfortable I feel talking to you."

"I don't' know if that's good or bad."

"It's definitely a good thing believe that. I'm gonna let you go. Enjoy your massage and make sure you get a chick, don't be having no dudes rubbing all over you."

"Yeah okay. I need some big strong hands in my life right now."

LatimaNicole

"Don't be fresh. Remember I'll hop on a red eye in a minute."

"Yeah yeah yeah. I'll talk to you later."

"Peace."

Cami couldn't believe that Matt opened up to her like that. Keisha always said she was a sucker for a sad story. She couldn't front Keisha might have been right. When Matt was telling her about his parents all she wanted to do was wrap her arms around him and give him a big hug.

Cani got back to the hotel and found Keisha sitting on the patio.

"Hey hun how was your nap?"

"Nap? Please. I called that husband of mine to let him know we made it here safe; of course I got the voicemail. He calls me back and wants a blow by blow description of what we're doing and who we're doing it with."

"You should've told him what happens in Malibu stays in Malibu."

"Yeah right you know that fool would be on the next thing smoking."

When You Love Somebody

"That's the same thing Matt said."

Aww damn, Cami thought, she slipped up and mentioned Matt's name.

"Matt? When did you speak to Matt?

"While I was out on the beach."

"Humph."

"Humph what?"

"Nothing."

"I know that look Keish, what's going on in that rock hard head of yours?"

"Nothing. I know you and I know Matt and if ya'll not careful somebody's gonna get hurt."

Cami mused, it might be too late for that. After their conversation she didn't think either one of them was going to be able to put an end to whatever this was.

"Keisha we just friends. Please what I want with a man with all that baggage? I wanna get married and have kids, Matt can't give me that."

"You know damn well things don't ever happen like we plan them. Shit if that was the case, I'd be on my second baby by now and Paul would have his shit together. It seems the older he gets the more immature he acts. He thinks I'm naïve and don't know what the fuck is going on but I ain't stupid. I know the man I married. Shit before Matt got married him and Paul used to do all type of shit in the street. I had chicks calling my phone, sitting outside the house and tearing up my car. When I finally had enough and was ready to leave his ass for good he proposed. When we got married I thought all that shit was behind us and then the music started taking off and that was all she wrote. He so caught up in that fake ass industry shit, he don't know his ass from his elbow. But you know all this so what am I telling you for? Anyway some people don't realize what they have until it's gone."

"You ain't never lied. That's what I told Hassan. You know all the drama I went through with him. After I finally put his ass out, he realized I was serious. Now he calls every day talking that baby please shit. The Negro had the nerve to tell me the reason

When You Love Somebody

why he was messing with that chick from Brooklyn was because I was all into my career and didn't have no time for him. Can you believe that shit? Anyway girl, enough about men. We came out here to relax and have a good time and that's what I plan to do."

"No doubt. Let's get this party started. I hope it's a fine ass dude giving me my massage. What are you laughing at?"

"Nothing let's go."

Keisha got her wish. After their mud wraps the attendant escorted them to a pair of open-air cabanas on the beach. It was really just a wooden canopy with silk fabric draped along the sides and tied to the four posts so that you had a view of the water from all sides. The fabric could be let down just in case you needed privacy. Waiting for them under the canopies, were two bare chested, tanned and buffed Adonises.

"Good afternoon ladies." Adonis number one said.

LatimaNicole

Keisha damn near tripped over herself and was about to bust her ass when Adonis number two caught her and helped her onto the massage table.

He said, "Ladies please get undressed, wrap your selves in the towels and lie face down on the table. We will be back shortly."

Keisha started waving her hands around like she was testifying in church.

"Lordy Ms. Claudy. Thank you Cami. Thank you. Thank you, thank you, thank you."

"Girl shut up and get undressed."

Adonis number one peeked in the curtain and asked, "Ladies are you ready?"

"Come on in." They said at the same time.

Cami was in heaven. The masseuses' hands were amazing. He was rubbing and kneading places that she had long ago forgotten about. He was working the inside of her thighs and she swore she was about to have an orgasm it felt so good.

Body: I wonder if Matt had hands like this.

When You Love Somebody

Mind: There you go Cami, cut it out you're gonna get yourself in trouble.

Body: I can't help it I'm so attracted to him.

Mind: Girl, get your shit together and just enjoy the massage.

Ummmm this is wonderful…she said to herself as she dosed off.

"Cami I've been wondering how good your body would feel and it's more than I could have ever imagined. Baby I just want to hold you is that okay?"

"Yes Matt."

"I want you so bad it hurts. Can I kiss you?"

"Yes."

"I want to taste every bit of you."

He started running his tongue up and down her neck while he was unbuttoning her jeans and putting his hands inside her panties.

"Can I taste you Cami?"

"Yes."

He stood over her and began to take his clothes off. She was watching thinking, damn this man is sexy as hell. He looked so

LatimaNicole

good in his Polo boxer briefs and wife
beater. If the bulge in his drawers was any
indication of what he was working with, he
definitely gave truth to the stereotype about
black men and penis sizes. As he continued
to strip he never took his eyes off of her.
His eyes were filled with so much desire that
Cami started to squirm on the bed. I felt like
he was fucking her with just his stare. Matt
laid down next to her and rubbed his feet up
and down her legs. YES! He took his socks
off! It was such a turn off for her when the
sex was about to go down and the dude took
off everything but his socks; that was so
disrespectful to her.

"Cami I don't know why I am so attracted to
you but I am and I don't want to hurt you.
Are you sure you want to do this?"

"Matt I'm a big girl and trust me I don't
want to be hurt. That shit don't tickle but it
is what it is. There's no turning back now."
As soon as she said that he put on a
Magnum XL condom, got on top of her and
rubbed his erect penis over her sweet spot.

When You Love Somebody

The shit was so long and thick she was thinking to herself there was no way he was going to fit that shit in her. But he took his time putting it in little by little while sucking on her nipples at the same time. By the time he finally got it all in, she was damn near begging him for it. He started massaging her pussy with long slow strokes and the shit felt so good that she couldn't control herself. Just when she thought that it couldn't get any better, he pulled out and buried his face in her pussy. She felt his tongue go completely flat while he licked her already swollen clit and again just when she was on the verge of exploding, he stopped and turned her over. She rose up on all fours and spread her legs in anticipation of him entering her from behind. He grabbed her legs and pulled her to the edge of the bed and stood up. Before he entered her he spread her ass cheeks apart and licked her from the crack of her ass to the opening of her pussy and she swore she was about to

LatimaNicole

climb the walls. She started screaming,

"Matt please give it to me."

He entered her with such force that she started shaking violently and uncontrollably.

"Matt I'm coming."

"I'm coming with you baby. Cccami you ffeel so goood."

"Oh yes Matt. Matt, Matt." She said while rocking back and forth on her knees.

He called out her name over and over again.

"Cami! Cami!"

She woke up and Keisha was sitting on the edge of the massage table calling her name.

"Damn Cami that Negro got you open. Every time you close your eyes you're dreaming about him. Normally I wouldn't say this, being a married woman, but you're gonna have to hit that so you can get that monkey off your back."

What the fuck! She was so embarrassed, her infatuation with Matt was getting out of hand.

"Yo Keish that dream was so crazy."

When You Love Somebody

"I'm sure it was." Keisha said while trying to hold in her laughter. "I know homey was bugging the fuck out. When they were leaving he said they left extra towels just in case we needed to clean up."

"Oh so you think that shit is funny huh?"

"Hilarious. Come on you horny toad, you could use a cold shower right about now."

Chapter 7
Camille

Cami hadn't spoken to Matt since Malibu. He called her a few times but she didn't returned any of his calls. She had made up her mind that she wouldn't allow herself to get caught up in a love triangle. She loved herself too much to settle for somebody else's man. Matt had too much going on and would never be able to give her the time and energy that she needed. She had to keep telling herself, "I don't do number two". That didn't mean she didn't think about him. She was still having those crazy dreams and on more than a few occasions, she had to pull the jack rabbit from under the bed and handle her business. Every time she spoke to Keisha she asked her if she'd spoken to him and it was getting on her nerves. Keisha had turned into his personal cheerleading squad. But Cami wasn't messing with Keisha or Matt. She

When You Love Somebody

had been going out on dates in an effort to keep herself busy and take her mind off of Matt, but the men she encountered were so corny. She met this one guy at a party and they had started talking. She asked him the usual questions, are you married or have a girlfriend, do you have any kids, do you still live with your mother etcetera. The asshole had the nerve to fix his face and say, "I have kids but I don't fuck wit them lil niggas cause they moms be buggin." Are you fucking serious? Cami thought. She swore she couldn't make that shit up.

She was getting ready to go to a Christmas party that one of her music industry clients was having at Cipriani's on forty-second street in Manhattan. To be honest she was not in the mood for the industry bullshit but work was work and she never turned down a gig. In that type of business you had to network to get your name out there and events like these were perfect for meeting potential clients. Cami stood in the middle of her walk in closet.

LatimaNicole

Deciding what to wear was proving harder than she thought. She usually liked to wear all black when she was working which helped her to be inconspicuous. Her attire usually consisted of a pair of jeans and some flats, but something told her she had better step it up a notch so she chose a black wool jersey Ralph Lauren dress that she bought when she and Keisha went shopping at Woodbury Commons. The dress fit like it was made for her. It was rare that she found dresses that fit well because of her small waist and wide hips. Either the top fit and the bottom was too tight or the bottom fit and the top was too big. This particular dress hugged all of her curves and the length was perfect for the suede Tory Burch boots she had gotten on sale from Neiman Marcus. She pulled her hair back into a bun, threw on a little lip-gloss and some mascara and called it a day. The car service picked her up on time, which was unbelievable. She had thought about driving but she really didn't want to be bothered with trying to

When You Love Somebody

find parking or paying an arm and a leg to park in a lot by Grand Central Station. It wasn't like she couldn't write it off as a business expense, but it was the principle of the thing. They had a hell of a nerve charging people forty or fifty dollars to park a friggin car!

The car turned onto forty-second street and there was a long line of black SUV's waiting to pull up to the front of the restaurant. She told the driver to drop her off at the corner and walked the rest of the way. Cipriani's was known for having some of the most beautiful architectural details and décor. It reminded her of one of those old banks you saw in movies with its sixty-five foot ceilings and marble columns. When she arrived at the door, she gave the attendant her name and he told her that she was to meet her client in the VIP area upstairs.

The VIP area was an entirely separate room from where the main party was being held. The spot where the celebrities would be partying. Cami met her client's assistant and she asked her if she needed anything. She told her no and began snapping pictures of the room. The atmosphere screamed wealth and she tried to capture that vibe with her camera. Once the party got into full swing she busied myself taking pictures while trying to be as incognito as possible. Her client, who was the VP of A&R for one of the most successful urban record labels in the country, motioned for her to join him at his table. She made it a rule not to mix business with pleasure but she knew he wasn't going to take no for an answer. So she went over and said hi. He introduced her to the people that were sitting at his table then grabbed her hand and kissed the back of it. Cami blushed as she pulled her hand back. She tried to excuse herself but he wasn't having it.

"Have a seat Camille. I am such a big fan of your work. You have a fantastic eye for photography. The photo spread you did for Vibe was incredible."

When You Love Somebody

"Thank you but I can't take all the credit. I worked with an amazing team."

"See that's what I like about you, you're so humble. Please take my personal number and give me a call. I would love to take you out to dinner sometime."

Cami couldn't believe her ears. This man was notorious in the industry for the amount of women he dated and ditched. He had a reputation for hooking up with women and then leaving them for the next young hottest thing on the scene. She took his number to be polite but she had no intentions of ever calling him. She said her goodbyes to everyone at the table and got back to work.

She got a shot of an up and coming R&B singer who had a huge hit over the summer, as she was walking in the door. Guess who was with her with his arms around her waist? That damn Paul. He just never stopped. She started to go over there and curse his ass out but she was working. She'd get at him later.

LatimaNicole

As the party started to wind down, she looked for her client's assistant to let her know that she was leaving when she felt somebody grab her elbow.

"Hi Cami."

Damn it was Matt. She didn't know why she didn't think that he would be there.

Especially since it was an industry party.

"Hi Matt, how are you?"

"Good now that I see you."

"That's good. How are the kids?"

"The kids are fine. Maya asked about you the other day. You know she's open over those pictures."

"She's so cute you better watch her."

"Trust me I'm all over her."

"It was good seeing you Matt. I'm calling it a night."

"Cami why haven't you returned any of my calls?"

"Matt you know why."

"Cami. I don't want nothing from you but your friendship. I like talking to you and I thought you felt the same way. I'm not

When You Love Somebody

trying to front and tell you that I'm not attracted to you. I think you know what time it is with that. But I'm a grown ass man and I know how to control myself. I would never try to disrespect you or run game on you, I don't get down like that."

"You're a good dude Matt and I definitely enjoyed our conversations but you and I both know the potential for us to cross the line is too great and I'm not willing to take that chance."

"I feel you and I respect that."

"Thank you. I guess I'll see you around."

"I was about to leave too. I just came to show my face. Did you drive?"

"No I took a cab."

"I'll take you home then."

"That's okay. I'll be fine."

"Cami come on it's not that serious. I promise I'll be on my best behavior. It doesn't make any sense for you to take a cab when we're both going back to Queens."

"How do you know I live in Queens?"

"I can't reveal my sources."

LatimaNicole

"Please the only person who could have told you is Don Juan de Dummy over there. I know he knows I see him. You would think he'd put some shade on his shit. But anyway, I'll ride with you just give me a minute to say my good byes."

"No doubt. Meet me downstairs."

Cami decided to go the bathroom before leaving and ran into Ms. Thang standing at the sink re-applying her lipstick. She had the dirty nerve to say, "I saw how you were looking at my man. Let me let you know right now, don't let this pretty face fool you, I gets down for mine. Trust me baby you are definitely out your league. Paul doesn't fuck with hired help."

It was taking everything Cami had in her not to slap the shit out of the slut but, being the bigger woman she put her in her place politely.

"Sweetheart let me explain something to you. Before you go around claiming niggas, you need to make sure they ain't spoken for already. That piece of shit that you willing

When You Love Somebody

to get your ass whooped for has been married to my cousin for the last fifteen years so you need to play your position before you get your young ass feelings hurt."

"Married? He never told me he was married."

"I bet he didn't."

Oh now the skank wanted to change her tone Cami thought as she shook her head. Please. Get the fuck out of here she said to herself as she walked in the stall and handled her business. When she came out old girl was gone and she washed her hands, freshened her lip gloss and met Matt downstairs. He must have read the look on her face because he mouthed, "What's wrong?"

She shook her head, said "nothing" and walked out of the door. When they got outside Matt said, "Cami, what up? Did somebody try to disrespect you?"

"Your boy is straight ridiculous with his shit. Would you believe that bird he up in there with had the nerve to step to me in the bathroom? Unfuckingbelievable! Talking about I saw how you was looking at my man. Is that trick serious?"

"Yo P is crazy but you know how he is so why are you surprised?"

"I'm not surprised. I'm just mad as hell. If he don't want to be married, then don't be. Be a man about your shit and leave. Him and Keisha been together since they were kids. If he ain't feeling it no more then move on. She don't deserve to be treated like that."

"I know but on the real, P can only do what Keisha allows him to do. She should have put her foot in his ass a long time ago."

The valet pulled up with the car and Matt opened Cami's door for her. She waited until he got in the car to let him have it.

"Oh so you telling me that it's Keisha's fault that Paul can't keep his dick in his pants?"

"Not at all. What I am saying is that Keisha ain't stupid. She knows the type of man she's working with. Paul is the type of nigga you have to make a believer out of.

When You Love Somebody

Until she puts her foot down he's not going to take her serious. She has to be willing to kick that dude to the curb if need be in order for him to get his shit together because he don't think he's doing anything wrong. In his mind as long as he takes care of her and she doesn't want for anything, then he's on his job and all that other shit don't have nothing to do with his marriage."

"I understand what you're saying but I'm tired of him making Keisha look like a fool, she's too good a woman for that."

"Trust me I know. I wish I had a Keisha at home."

No he didn't say that. That's the first time he had made any reference to his wife.

"I met my wife when she was fifteen. Of course I didn't know she was that young, she lied and said she was eighteen. I'ma keep it funky, she was a jump off. At the time I was trying to make it in the industry and I was still getting money in the street. I wasn't trying to be tied down but I had a couple of chicks that I fucked with for different reasons. Me and my man used to bag up in her crib when her Moms was at work. I would have her transport shit for me from time to time when I couldn't find anybody else. Long story short, she popped up pregnant. At first I was like whatever, I knew she was fucking other niggas in the hood so it probably wasn't mine anyway. But since she was blaming it on me, I played her close 'til she had the baby and even though he looked just like me, I still had a DNA test done. When it came back that he was definitely mine, I married her. I always promised myself that if I had a seed, I would be a better parent than my parents were. So I stopped running around in the streets and focused on the music. When I wasn't on the road I made sure that I was home every night to put my little man to bed and that he saw my face every morning when he woke up."

This was the reason why Cami was feeling this dude. He was so honest and open about things and it was turning her on.

When You Love Somebody

"Do you love her?"

"I love her but I'm not in love with her. She's my kid's mother so I'm always going to have love for her, but as far as being in love with her, I don't think I ever was."

"Doesn't that bother you?"

"At first it didn't because this was the choice I made and I was doing it for my kids not her. She has her shit with her but I don't let it bother me because my kids are what matters to me the most."

"But don't you think you're setting the wrong example for your kids? Children are very intuitive and they pick up on things we don't even realize. Don't you know that kids pattern their relationships after their parents'?

"Trust me I know. That's why I try to talk to them and be honest about what's going on with me and their Mom. I'm not mad at the shit my wife does. I understand she never really had a childhood because she got pregnant when she was so young but at the same time it was her choice. A couple of years after Sonny was born she told me that she put a hole in the condom that's why she was so sure it was mine. So she deliberately got pregnant in order to trap me and to some extent it worked. She knew I was a good dude and I wasn't gonna shit on her so now she does her because she's comfortable with the fact that I ain't going nowhere."

"Wow! And you're okay with that?"

"Like I said Cami. It is what it is. I made my bed and I'm lying in it. I'm not going to have my babies suffer because their Moms can't get it together."

"But don't you think they're suffering anyway?"

"Suffering? No, but they definitely know that our family is not like their friends. The other day Misa said to me that one of the kids in her class asked her did she have a mother. I know that's because she never takes them to or picks them up from school. She doesn't really fuck with the kids at all on a day to day basis. She's there for birthdays and other holidays but she's not

When You Love Somebody

the one to get up and take the girls shopping or get their hair done and shit like that. But she's young. She was sixteen when she had Sonny and then here come Maya and Misa so she never really got to enjoy her life. Plus in the beginning I was on the road a lot and she had to hold the baby down. Her Moms wasn't no help. Shit she was young too out there trying to get her groove on. Now that I'm behind the scenes and can spend more time at home she's taking that as her cue to do her."

"But what about you Matt? Don't you think you deserve happiness? If you're not happy, how do expect to make your kids happy? After a while it's going to take a toll on you and you're going to start to look elsewhere to have your needs met."

"Real talk. I've been so focused on the kids and the music; I haven't had time to dwell on it. Until I met you. You know how they say you can't miss what you don't have until somebody lets you borrow it"

"I've never heard that before but okay."

LatimaNicole

"I just made it up." Matt said with that killer smile of his.

"Cami, I've never been able to have conversations like this with my wife. We're just not on the same page. Would you believe we've been married for nine years and have never been on vacation or even out to dinner just the two of us?"

"That's crazy Matt. Life is too short to live like that. What's going to happen when the kids grow up and leave home" You're going to wake up one day and realize you wasted the best years of your life and then it will be too late."

"I know Cami. But what am I supposed to do? What exit do I get off?"

What a way to change the subject. "Get off at Springfield Boulevard."

"Got you. Thank you Cami."

"What are you thanking me for?

"I don't know it just felt like the right thing to say.

"I should be thanking you."

"For what?"

When You Love Somebody

"For letting down your guard and being yourself with me. Most of the men I run into are so busy trying to front and be something that they're not that it's ridiculous. I'm not impressed by material things because they're not permanent. I make my own money and I don't need anyone to take care of me. Don't get me wrong it's nice to be taken care of and I don't have a problem taking care of my man if he's taking care of me. I don't date men because of what they have or what they appear to have because we both know everything that glitters and gold."

"I feel you on that one."

"Well thanks for the ride."

Matt got out and opened the car door for Cami.

"Cami can I walk you to your door?"

"I'm a big girl Matt. I think I can make it from the curb to the door."

One of the reasons Cami chose her townhouse condo was because of the neighborhood. She lived in an upper middle

LatimaNicole

class section of Queens called Bayside. If it
wasn't for the fact that her condo was a
foreclosure she never would have been able
to afford to live there. Her neighbors were
mostly doctors, lawyers and executives,
which is a world away from where she grew
up.

"But if it will make you feel better you can
wait until I get in the house before you pull
off."

"What would make me feel better is you
inviting me in so we can finish our
conversation."

"Now why would I want to do that? That
would be like playing with fire."

"Why you say that? I promise to be on my
best behavior."

"I'm sure you do."

She hoped she didn't regret her decision.
She was banking on him having more self-
control than her, if not they were in trouble.

"Welcome to casa de Cami," she said while
dramatically sweeping her arm across the
air, "have a seat. I'm gonna go put my

When You Love Somebody

camera away. If you want something to drink the kitchen is to your left." She changed her clothes while she was upstairs and came down wearing an old NYU sweat suit and a pair of thick socks.

"You okay Matt?"

"Yeah I was just admiring your artwork. Did you take all of these pictures?"

"Yes."

"They're hot. I'm really feeling the one of the little kids in the sprinklers."

"I took that when I was going to NYU. I was trying to capture the innocence of the moment."

"You definitely succeeded. You're very talented Cami."

"Thank you. Did you get anything to drink?"

"Nah. I didn't want to be roaming around in your kitchen."

"Do you want anything? I think I have some Heinekens in there."

"That's okay. I don't drink beer and plus I have to drive so I'll take some juice or water."

"Okay, but I'm going to have a glass of wine."

"Do your thing I'm straight."

Cami brought her glass into the living room, passed Matt a bottle of water and sat on the couch with a sigh.

"Long day?"

"Not really but it's something about coming home that makes me get into instant relax mode."

"Your crib is definitely relaxing. Shit I could fall asleep right here in this chair this shit is so comfortable."

Humph I would rather you fall asleep in my bed she mumbled under her breath.

"Everybody says that when they come here for the first time. But I have to be comfortable in my home. There is so much shit going on in the world that you are forced to deal with, I think your home

When You Love Somebody

should be the one place you can relax, relate and release. Your sanctuary."

"No question. You got any movies?"

"I'm not really a movie person but I have a few old school classics. Look under the table and take your pick."

"9 ½ weeks? What's that about?"

That was the last movie she should be watching with him. It was straight erotic with all the sex scenes, so she lied and said, "It's a chick flick you don't want to watch that."

"I know what the movie is about I just wanted to see what you was gonna say. Let me find out you be getting your freak on. On the real though I'll pass on that one."

He picked up Penitentiary, put it in the DVD player and then sat next to her on the couch.

"Cami can you turn off the lights?"

Hell no she said to herself. Is this Negro crazy? She can barely stand sitting next to him with all the lights on let alone in the dark, but she didn't want him to think he had her under pressure so she got up and

LatimaNicole

dimmed the lights. She had forgotten how
funny this movie was. The scene where Too
Sweet beats the hell out of Half Dead while
the midget and the prostitute were under the
boxing ring getting busy cracked her up
every time she saw it. By the time the
movie ended it was four in the morning and
for some reason she was hungry as hell.
Cami got up, turned on the lights and asked
Matt if he would like something to eat. As
she was walking to the kitchen he got up and
followed her.

"How about you get dressed and we go to
the diner and get some breakfast."

"Get dressed? I am dressed. All I have to do
is put my sneakers on. What's the matter?
You don't like my sweats?"

"Trust me Ma, you look good in anything
you put on, but I know how ya'll women
are. If you're okay, I'm okay."

"Well then let's go."

She put her wineglass in the sink and when
she turned around Matt was standing behind
her.

When You Love Somebody

"Cami to be honest, I would rather have you for breakfast."

"Matt I thought you were going to behave."

"I'm trying" he said grabbing her by the waist, "but you're making it so hard for a brother." He put his hand around the back of her neck and started kissing her like he was trying to devour her mouth. At first she resisted but she couldn't deny the heat that was rising in her pelvic area so she gave in. They were standing in the kitchen groping and rubbing on each other like a bunch of teenagers, when Matt picked Cami up and sat her on top of the counter. He looked at her and said, "Cami I want you so bad it's driving me crazy, but if you don't want to do this I can leave."

Was this dude crazy? He wasn't going anywhere. She answered him by sucking on his bottom lip. He picked her up again and this time she wrapped her legs around his waist. He kissed her on the forehead and said, "Can we take a shower together?"

LatimaNicole

"My bedroom is the double doors facing the stairs."

They undressed each other and headed to the bathroom. Fuck a shower, I'm ready now was all that was running through Cami's mind. She didn't want to seem hard up so she let him take the lead. He lathered up the shower pouf and slowly wash between her thighs and around the outside of her vagina. He spread her lips apart and gently used the pouf to bring her about two seconds from an orgasm. She didn't know how much more of it she could stand. Matt washed her up real slow and seductive like he was committing every inch of her body to his memory. The boy definitely had skills. Every part of her body was on fire and it was not from the steam. She wanted to grab his penis and just put it in herself but she checked herself and turned the tables on him by washing in between his legs making sure to pay special attention to his ass and balls. After what seemed like an eternity of torture they got out of the shower and made it to the bed.

When You Love Somebody

She had to admit, Matt had an amazing body. She thought about D'Angelo in that video where he's standing in front of the camera with no shirt on and his skin glistening. But D'Angelo didn't have anything on Matt. Cami thought it was so sexy how his stomach muscles formed a V pointing to his penis. Which by the way was standing at full attention curve and all. She hoped all the anticipation was worth it.

"Cami do you have any condoms?"

She looked in the nightstand drawer praying that there was at least one. To her relief there was a three pack. She gave Matt the condoms; he took one out of the box and said, "I want you to put in on me."

She tore the package open and rolled the condom on to his rock hard dick making sure she left some room at the tip, they didn't need any accidents. Matt turned Cami over and started kissing her down her back. When he got to her butt cheeks he spread them apart and blew in her ass. She felt like screaming so she grabbed the pillow and bit down on it. She swore she was about to pass out, she was so turned on. He lifted her up onto her knees and finally put it in. Cami sighed as he entered her because the sensation felt so good. Between the shower and the ass blowing her pussy was so wet she could feel her juices dripping down her thigh. Matt was taking his time with her but she was so hot and horny that she started bucking like a prize winning stallion. She said, "Matt grab my ankles." He grabbed her ankles and she took off. Matt let her take the lead for a while alternating between moaning and calling her name, then he grabbed her by the waist and slowed it down. He thrust in and out so slow and deliberate that she could feel every inch of his crooked circumcised dick.

"Cami you feel so good. I want all of you. Can I have all of you Cami?"

"Take it Matt. You want this pussy take it baby."

He squeezed her ass cheeks and said, "give it to me baby."

When You Love Somebody

She tightened her muscles and started rocking back and forth on her knees. Matt was behind her moaning and groaning like he was in pain. He grabbed her hair and said, "Baby here I come." Cami sped up the rhythm and then it hit her. Her pussy started to contract and then it felt like a dam burst inside of her. Her orgasm was so intense that her knees buckled and she fell flat on her stomach. Matt fell on top of her and laid there breathing like he had just run a marathon. He rolled over to the other side of the bed and Cami turned onto her back. He kissed her and said, "What the fuck girl? You dangerous."

She just looked at Matt not saying anything as the weight of what just happened hit her like a ton of bricks.

"What's the matter Cami?"

"We fucked up Matt."

"I don't know about the up part but there was definitely some fucking going on."

"You know what I mean."

LatimaNicole

"I know but I don't want to think about that right now. Let's just enjoy each other, we'll work it out later come here."

He took her in his arms and kissed her forehead.

"I know my situation is not ideal but it is what it is. Believe me I never intended for this to happen but when I'm around you I can't help myself. I know I shouldn't be here with you right now but I can't think of any place I'd rather be."

"Matt I don't know you like that so I can't tell whether you're being honest or running game but for some reason I trust you and I feel safe with you. Just promise me that whatever happens you will always be honest with me. If you need to fall back I understand but just communicate that to me."

"Like I told you Cami, I'm not trying to hurt you. I don't know what's in store but I do know that I want us to be friends regardless of whether or not we ever do this again."

"So what now Matt?"

When You Love Somebody

He looked at her and started grinning.

"Round two."

Chapter 8

Matthew

Matt drove home from Cami's thinking he had really fucked up. How did he let himself give in to temptation? It just felt so right to him and the reality was he didn't want to leave. If it wasn't for the kids, he would have stayed in bed with Cami for the rest of the weekend. He knew he had to stay focused. He couldn't let this thing with Cami get out of hand, couldn't let a piece of pussy having him screw up his priorities. He pulled up to the crib and Louise was getting out of her girlfriend's car. It was like 7:30 in the morning and she was just getting home.

"What up Wee you just getting in?"

She was shocked as hell to see him. She probably thought he would be holed up in the studio by now.

"Yeah, me and my girls went to a party in Jersey and then out to breakfast. What you doin just getting in?"

When You Love Somebody

"Ya boy P got drunk at the party and I had to play chaperone. I drove him home then had to take a cab back to the city to get my car."

"Oh okay. Paul know he don't need to be drinking like that. Good thing you was there."

"True."

He knew she was lying about the party shit but he wondered if she knew he was lying. Probably not, she was so wrapped up in her bullshit,that it probably never occurred to her that he could be out fucking around. It was a good thing the kids were over her sister's house for the weekend. Maybe they could get a chance to talk without the conversation turning into an argument.

By the time he pulled the car in the garage and made it upstairs, she was already in bed. He was tired as hell but he couldn't sleep so he took a shower and headed downstairs to the studio. Matt came up with some of the most banging tracks when he had shit on his mind. He threw on a beat he'd been

working on and just zoned out to the music.
For some reason he had been in a real old
school mood lately. He searched through I-
tunes for some stuff he could sample and
came across a joint by the Isley Brothers
called "Sensuality Pt. 1&2." He
downloaded it and leaned back in his chair.
The instrumental on the joint was sick.
'Every day I Dream' huh. The song made
him think about Cami. What the fuck did he
just do? He asked himself. Damn that girl
had him open. She was all he thought about.
Every woman he'd ever been with had
always wanted something from him, Louise
included. But Cami was different. He
connected with her on a level that scared the
shit out of him. Maybe it was because he
could be himself with her. He didn't have to
worry about making sure that she was taken
care of. There was no pressure to always be
grinding. Plus she was a dime piece. He
loved to see her walk in a room with her
hips swaying. She thought she was doin
something putting those sweatpants on. But

When You Love Somebody

you couldn't hide a body like that no matter what you put on. On the real, Cami was everything Louise was not. She had her head on straight, she was mad talented and down to earth. Some women who be talking that independent shit, don't know how to let a man be the man in their relationship. They wanted to do everything and as soon as you fell back and let them, they were quick to tell you they didn't need you.

Matt looked at the clock on his Mac, it was ten o'clock already, he needed to try to get a couple of hours sleep in before the kids got home. He went upstairs and heard Louise on the phone with one of her skank ass home girls. The way the master suite was set up, when you walked through the double doors you entered sitting area first. Once you walked past the sitting area, the master bathroom was on the left and walk-in closets on the right. The carpet was so thick that Louise didn't hear him come in. He sat on the velvet sofa and heard her being real reckless with her mouth.

LatimaNicole

"He told me Paul got drunk and he had to drive him home. Yeah I believe him. Please that Nigga ain't goin nowhere. Ain't no chick gonna deal with all his luggage. Anyway he start actin like he creeping, I'll conveniently forget to get my birth control shot and put another hole in the condom. Baby number four would straighten his ass right on out. You know how feel about his kids."

"Girl I ain't crazy, I'm just keepin it real." He couldn't believe what he'd heard. This broad really had it twisted. She must have thought he was some punk ass Nigga. He felt like smackin cold shit outta her. She was lucky he didn't hit women. Matt let Louise's comments roll off his back. He walked out of the room and slammed the door behind him just to let her know he heard her ass.

He went and laid down in Sonny's room to get some sleep. He'd deal with the bullshit later. His first instinct was to call Cami but he fell back.

When You Love Somebody

When he woke up Sonny was standing over him.

"Daddy what you doing in my room?"

"What up Sonny? I was tired and your Mom kept yappin on the phone so I came in here to get some rest."

"Dad can I ask you a question?"

"Of course."

"What would you do if you found out Mommy was cheating on you?"

Where the fuck did that come from he thought.

"I don't know Sonny. That's a hard one. I guess we would try to figure it out and do what's best for the family. Why do you ask?"

"Because this boy named Benji in my class said his Mom cheated on his Dad and now his Dad don't live with them no more. I don't want you to move out if Mom ever cheats on you."

"Come here Sonny. No matter what happens between me and your Mom, nothing will change the fact that I love you

and your sisters more than I love myself. I
promise you that no matter what I will
always be there for ya'll. Trust me, in a
couple of years you probably won't even
like me."

"Nah Dad you the coolest old dude I know
besides Uncle P."

"Old, who you calling old?"

"Come on Dad you like thirty-five that's
ancient."

"I'll show you who's ancient, meet me in
the driveway and let this old dude school
you on some b-ball."

Damn, Sonny got Matt to thinking. Was he
really doing what was best for his kids by
trying to stay with Louise? Kids were so
damn smart these days; they picked up on
everything. They probably knew shit wasn't
right with him and their Louise. They
needed to get their shit together. The older
the kids got the more they were gonna see
and understand that something wasn't right.
He decided to give Cami a call to see what
she had planned for the day.

When You Love Somebody

"Hello."

"Hey Cami."

"Good morning hun. How are you today?"

"Good and you."

"I'm alright. A bit tired. Good thing today is my day off."

"No doubt. Why are you so tired?"

"Umm because I had company last night and they acted like they didn't want to leave."

"Is that right?

"Yes it is. So what's on your agenda for today seeing as though you're full of energy?"

"Nothing much. Me and Sonny just finished playing basketball. I'll probably hang out with the kids for a minute and then finish up this track I was working on this morning."

"You were able to go in the studio when you left here? I would have thought my performance would have been the only session you needed."

"True. But you know how it is when something or someone inspires you."

LatimaNicole

"Oh so you're saying I inspired you? Hold on let me get my helmet because you're about to hit me in the head with some BS."

"Never that. On the real though, I just wanted to holla at you before I started making moves for the day."

"Okay. Be good."

"I think I showed you how good I could be last night."

"I have no idea what you're talking about."

"Yeah okay. I'll talk to you later."

"Peace."

Matt got up to go see what his rugrats were doing because they were too quiet. Maya met him at the door and said, "Daddy, Mommy said to tell you she went to the mall and to ask you what's for dinner cause she didn't feel like cooking."

What else was new he thought to himself.

"What do you want for dinner?"

"Can we go to Friendly's?"

"Well Missy, whatever you want from Friendly's we can make right here at home;

When You Love Somebody

so go get your brother and sister and ya'll come help me cook."

She stood on her tip toes and yelled at the top of her lungs, "Sonny, Misa, Daddy said come in the kitchen."

"Maya stop yelling and go find them."

"Sorry Daddy."

Matt's cell phone rang and the Caller ID said it was from an unknown number.

"Hello."

"This is Sprint. You have a collect call from 'Bill' an inmate in a correctional facility. Press one to accept the charges, press two to reject this call or just hang up."

He pressed one and his Dad's voice came over the line.

"What's up young blood?"

"Hey Pop how's it going?"

"Same soup different bowl. Everything is everything. How's my Grandkids?"

"Being brats as usual."

"You can't blame nobody but yourself. I told you before you give them kids too much."

LatimaNicole

"Yeah I know but I can't help it. I want them to have the things I didn't when I was growing up."

"Listen, I know I let you down and if I knew back then what I know now, I would have done a lot of things differently. I can't dwell on the past and you can't let the past dictate your future. If you want them kids to have a chance in life you gotta stop spoiling them. If you hand everything to them they're going to go through life looking for handouts and never appreciate the value of hard work and struggle."

"I know Pop. Trust me I spoil them but I also teach them responsibility. I do admit that sometimes I go overboard to compensate for their Moms not being involved like she should but it is what it is."

"I don't know your wife, all I have to go by is what you've told me but seems to me she needs to get her mind right and so do you. Don't you know kids pattern their relationships after their parents'? I can tell you married an emotionally distant woman

When You Love Somebody

because that's what you experienced
growing up with your Mom. Now I'm going
to tell you something about your mother that
you probably didn't know. When I met her I
had just come back from Nam and was
looking for work. She worked part-time in a
store called Alexander's on Queens
Boulevard. I went there to buy me a suit to
wear on job interviews and she helped me
pick out a nice one. I knew she was a little
young but I wanted to take her out anyway.
I used to show up at the store every day for
about a month before she finally let me take
her out. Now mind you I still didn't have a
job but I managed to borrow some money
and we went to see a movie at the movie
theater on Jamaica Avenue. Afterwards we
walked down to King Park and sat on a
bench and talked. She told me she was
going to school to be a teacher and this was
her last year. Well to make a long story
short we hit it off and the next thing you
know we were together like peanut butter
and jelly. She graduated and started teaching

LatimaNicole

while she went to school at night to get her master's but meanwhile I couldn't find a job. This country turned its back on cats coming home from the war especially us black soldiers. I was messed up behind that and started being in the street running numbers and selling dope. A lot of dudes got hooked on that heron overseas so I was making a nice piece of change. When your mom got pregnant with you, she tried to push me to marry her but I got scared and bucked. Man I wasn't ready for no family, I didn't have my shit together to be taking care of a family. I know me not being around like I should have broke her heart but I was selfish. She tried any and everything she could to make me come back but by that time I was so out there in the streets that nothing else mattered.

Man I was making money hand over fist in those days. I would come by, mostly at night and drop off a few ducketts but your mom wouldn't take it. She wanted me to get my shit together and come home but I was

When You Love Somebody

so far out there that nothing mattered but me making that money. I knew I was wrong for turning my back on ya'll but them streets had a hold on me man. I was making more money than I had ever seen and had access to the best that money could buy, even women."

"Pop you don't have to explain yourself to me. That's old news. My Mom's gave me the low down before she died. I know one thing though, she really loved you man. Even though she was strung out and the cancer ate her up, I always felt like she died of a broken heart."

"I'm sorry son if I could rewind and go back I would do so many things differently. You don't know how much I blame myself for your mother's death. I knew she wasn't strong which is why I tried to keep her away from the street life. When I found out she was getting high it damn near killed me but what could I do by that time I was getting high my damn self."

LatimaNicole

"For what it's worth I don't blame you. We all make mistakes."

You have sixty seconds

"Well son give my grandbabies a hug for me and tell them granddad will see them real soon. I'll try to call on Friday."

"Ok Pop stay up."

Matt hung up the phone with his dad and thought about their conversation. Did he really want to get to be my pops age and look back at his life full of regret?

"Daddy I'm hungry" Misa's little fat fingers pulling on his pants leg brought him back to reality.

"What you want to eat mama?"

"I want ice cream and chicken."

"Ice cream and chicken? Where did you get that from? How about we have chicken for dinner and then we can go to Coldstone for some ice cream okay?"

"K daddy."

He didn't understand how any parent could choose not to be a part of their children's

When You Love Somebody

lives. His kids were the best things to ever happen to him.

Chapter 9

Camille

"So Camille, let's talk about why
you think you're attracted to emotionally
unavailable men."

Cami was sitting in her therapist's office
about to wrap up her monthly visit when Dr.
Washington dropped that can of worms in
her lap. She had started seeing a therapist
two years ago because she kept having panic
attacks and needed to get to the root of the
problem. Dr. Washington helped her to
realize that a lot of her issues stemmed from
the murders of her parents when she was a
kid.

She remember it like it was yesterday. She
had gone over to her grandparent's house to
spend the weekend with Keisha. At about
2:30 in the morning the phone rang and she
could hear my grandmother scream noooo
so loud that she woke up the neighbors.
Cami's next door neighbor had called to say
that somebody broke into their house and

When You Love Somebody

shot her parents. She knew something was wrong but her grandmother wouldn't tell her. She just said her neighbor Mrs. Cooper was coming to stay with her and Keisha so she and granddad could go to the hospital. Cami called her best friend who lived next door to her and she told her that her parents were dead. She said somebody ran up in the house looking for her dad's money and drugs. They shot her dad in the head execution style and her mom in the chest. The cops said she must have walked in on the thieves because her body was found in the hallway and dad's was tied to a chair. When Cami got older, she found out that her dad ran a very lucrative drug business and had made a lot of enemies while doing so. The killers, however were guys from her dad's crew that were jealous of the amount of money he was making and decided they weren't getting enough of the pie. Cami was in shock and couldn't stop shaking. She stayed up the whole night shaking and rocking back and forth. Keisha

LatimaNicole

and Mrs. Cooper tried to console her but there was nothing they could do or say. Her life had been turned upside down in the blink of an eye and she was devastated. Her parents were her world. She was truly a daddy's girl. She never wanted for anything. Looking back she realized how much her parents spoiled her. She was the only child and had the best of everything. She remembered for her tenth birthday her mom hired an interior designer and a graffiti artist to redecorate her room. Her cousins were so jealous. Even the kids in school were jealous because she wore the latest designer fashions. One Christmas her dad bought her a mink jacket and a pair of diamond earrings. They didn't use material things to show how much they loved her though. Some of her best memories were of them sitting on the couch in their pajamas watching movies and eating popcorn. Her dad used to make her sit in the middle of her parents and when he thought she was falling

When You Love Somebody

asleep, he would take a feather and run it under her nose or tickle her ear with it.

Her parent's death affected her in ways that that she just beginning to realize.

"So how did things change for you after your parents died?"

"My whole world came crashing down. I was my parents' baby girl. I never had to share them with anyone. Not only did I get all of their love and attention, they showered me with gifts just because. I went from having my own room and a closet full of designer clothes, to living with my grandparents and sharing a room with my cousin Keisha. My grandparents were from the old school and they didn't believe in that kind of excess. Living with them was quite an adjustment."

The panic attacks and anxiety that she was suffering from according to her therapist was a result of the trauma she suffered as a child. The fact that she suppressed her feelings about her parents' murders did little to help the situation. Dr. Washington even had her thinking that their deaths also affected her relationships with men. She had a tendency to attract emotionally unavailable men because sub consciously, she was emotionally unavailable herself. Truth be told she was scared to get into a relationship for fear of the person leaving her and her having to relive that pain from her parents' deaths.

"Ok Cami our time is up. I want you to think about my question. I noticed how cleverly you avoided it."

"I will Dr. Washington."

"Will I see you next month?"

"Yes. I'll make an appointment with Stacey."

Cami grabbed her things and left the doctor's office in a hurry. She checked her messages as she left the doctor's office and the first message she retrieved was from Keisha cursing her out.

"Okay heifer I don't know what the hell is going on with you but I haven't heard from

When You Love Somebody

you in a couple of months. You need to get your shit together and call me."

Cami hadn't seen or spoken to Keisha since Christmas. In all honesty she felt like a hypocrite, as much as she got on Paul about his cheating, she had some nerve screwing a married man. She felt she was no better than the broads he ran around with. Even though she didn't intentionally set out to start seeing Matt- it just kind of happened-she knew from the very beginning that he was married and had every opportunity to put the brakes on the affair. With that being said, she felt her situation couldn't be compared to the shit Paul did. However, cheating was cheating no matter how you looked at it. She was so torn. How did she let this happen? She knew better but just couldn't help herself. No matter how many times she told herself that nothing good was going to come out of their relationship and to nip it in the bud, she found herself calling him, needing him. Fuck! She was an emotional wreck. Good thing she had work to keep her occupied or she'd really be in bad shape.

She needed to call Keisha so they could talk.

"Hello."

"Hey Keish what's up?"

"Don't wassup me, where the fuck you been?"

"I've been busy with work. I've been meaning to come by but I haven't had the chance."

"Yeah fucking right. This is me you're talking to. The only time I don't hear from you is when you're stressing about something. So are you gonna tell me or do I have to beat it outta you?"

"I don't know what you're talking about. I'm good. Just trying to take my career to the next level. I've been working on a book of my photographs and teaching at Parson's two nights a week."

Well at least that wasn't a total lie.

"That's great Cami. When did you get the teaching gig?"

"It started off on a trial basis and then they offered me an adjunct position. At first I

When You Love Somebody

didn't know if I wanted to do it but I'm glad
I did I really like it."

"Unhuh sounds good."

"Unhuh what?"

"Oh nothing just remember I know you
better than you know yourself and you
should know that whatever it is I got your
back. We're sister cousins and nothing or no
one is going to get in the way of that."

"Well alright Mrs. Carl Thomas so
emotional-where did all that come from?"

"I don't know. I guess this is what they
mean when they say pregnancy and
hormones turn women into a big bag of
emotions."

"What the fuck did you just say?"

"What? That I'm an emotional wreck?

"Don't play with me heifer!"

"Well if you weren't hibernating and
returned calls sometimes you would know
that I'm sixteen weeks pregnant."

"Oh my goodness Keish I'm so happy for
you."

LatimaNicole

"Thank you. I haven't told a lot of people yet because I wanted to wait until I got out of my first trimester. I'm in the first week of my second trimester and everything looks good so far."

"But I've spoken to you since then, why didn't you tell me?"

"Hell I didn't find out until I was almost 8 weeks. I counted back and it must have happened when we came back from Cali. Paul was on his I love my wife shit and was all over me."

That was just like Paul, as soon as he felt like Keisha might be leaving his trifling ass, he made it a point to be Mr. Ronnie Romance.

"Oh my goodness I have to come see you. Are you showing yet? Has the baby started moving? Do you know what you're having?"

"Oh now you wanna be all concerned, but when I was trying to call you to tell your monkey ass you wouldn't return my calls."

"I said I was sorry."

When You Love Somebody

"You know what they say about being sorry. Don't let it happen again."

"Alright already. You're not a mother yet so slow your row home girl. I'm not teaching tonight so I'm gonna come see you. I have so much to tell you."

As soon as she hung up with Keisha her phone rang. She looked at the caller ID and saw Matt's number and immediately broke into a smile.

"Hey babe."

"Wassup baby girl how's your day so far?"

"It's going great. I just found out that Keisha and Paul are going to have a baby."

"Oh word! P didn't even tell me."

"Yeah they didn't tell anyone until she went past her first trimester."

"That's what's up. How she doing?"

"She and the baby are fine. What's up with you? Are we still on for dinner?"

"Of course. I was thinking that I'd cook for you. I know you're a picky eater but I throws down in the kitchen and your picky ass won't be able to resist my food."

LatimaNicole

"Whatever. You think you the bomb huh?"

"Yup that's why you love me."

"Nobody said anything about loving your cocky ass."

"It's cool I love you too babe."

Whoa where did that come from did he just mention the L word?

"Matt don't say things just because you think that's what I want to hear. We haven't been friends long enough to be talking about love."

"Cami please don't tell me what I mean and don't mean. I know what I said and I meant it and what's with this friends bullshit? Is that all I am to you is your friend?"

"Okay so if we're not friends what are we?"

"I thought we were in a relationship but I guess I was wrong."

Relationship? Was he fucking kidding? How the hell could they be in a relationship if he's married? The man had lost his damn mind.

"Matt let me ask you this, if we were out together and you had to introduce me, how

When You Love Somebody

would you do that? What would you introduce me as?"

There was a pause on the line and Cami could tell that Matt had never thought about that before and was trying to come up with an answer to back up his argument.

"Cami I know our situation ain't the best but it is what it is. You're my woman and I'm your man so you can dead that friend shit."

This boy must have bumped his head Cami thought to herself. Woman? His woman?

"Come again."

"I'm saying I ain't seeing nobody other than Louise and we ain't even rocking like that. She does her thing and I'm doing mine. And you better not be seeing nobody else."

"Excuse me."

"You heard what I said woman. I'm dead ass Cami. You're not going nowhere and neither am I."

"Think about this. What would you say to Maya or Misa if they came home with a married man? How would you feel?"

LatimaNicole

"I would tell them that they're setting themselves up to get hurt and that it's wrong to come in between another woman's marriage. I would also tell them that they are too beautiful and too special to have to share a man with someone else."

Well damn that bit of honesty was like a slap in the face. She appreciated Matt for being so honest but now she felt like shit.

"So if you love me like you say you do why wouldn't you want the same for me?"

"Our situation is different Cami. I'm only married on paper. I didn't get married for love. I married Louise because I didn't want to have any bastard babies. Truthfully, I don't think she ever loved me either. She was probably just looking for a come up and getting pregnant was her way of making sure that she would always be taken care of."

"So if you knew that why did you marry her? You could have given your kids your last name without getting married."

When You Love Somebody

"I don't expect you to understand but I want you to know that I've never loved a woman the way I love you. What we have is much more than an affair. To be honest when I'm going about my day it's you I think about. When I'm out and about it's you that I want to call to tell about my day. If I'm in the mall I don't say oh that would look nice on Louise, I'm thinking about what I can get for you. When I'm finished in the studio I can't wait to call you and see how your day went."

Matt was everything Cami always wanted in a man. He treated her like a Queen and he was right. For someone on the outside looking in you would think they had the perfect relationship. They had so much fun together and he was not only her lover, he was her friend. They could talk to each other about anything. Even though he was married, she never felt like he would lie to her or try to run game on her. He'd always been honest about his situation. She didn't have to worry about any drama from his wife, he'd managed to keep that part of his life separate from theirs and she appreciated that.

"Matt I know you're trying to make me feel better but this is something I'm gonna have to work out on my own. We're just gonna have to take this one day at a time and see how it plays out. But at some point you're gonna have to make a decision."

"All I ask is that you be patient with me baby. I know you deserve much more than I can offer you right now but I promise I will never do anything to hurt you intentionally. Don't worry we'll work it out. Let me finish up here and I'll see you later oaky."

"Okay. What time should I expect you for dinner?"

"Probably around 8. You want me to come to the house or the studio?"

"Come to the house. I'll meet you there. I have to go see Keisha first."

"Cool, I'll see you soon and Cami don't worry we'll work it out."

When You Love Somebody

Cami wanted to make sure that everything was in place for her date with Matt tonight. He had been coming on strong these last couple of weeks and tonight Cami was sure that she was going to break it off with him. She just hoped that she would be able to resist his charms long enough to have him hear her out. The stress of falling in love with Matt was taking a toll on her mentally and physically and she wanted so bad to get off the roller coaster ride that her emotions seemed to be on lately.

When dinner was done Matt called her to the dining room table. She took a deep breath, sat down and immediately began to rattle off the speech she had been practicing all day.

"Matt I can't do this anymore," Camille said as she looked down at her plate.

"Do what? Eat your dinner?"

"Us, I can't do us anymore."

"What are you talking about Cami?"

"I deserve more than what you can give me right now. Seeing Keisha earlier made me realize that I want a family of my own too.

LatimaNicole

Why can't I have the fairy tale wedding, the 2.5 kids and the picket fence?"

Matt put his head in his hands and stayed in that position for what seemed like an eternity. When he looked up he said, "You deserve that and more and I'm gonna spend the rest of my life making sure you never want for anything. I keep telling you Cami you're my woman and you're not going anywhere."

Cami looked at Matt as if he had just said the stupidest thing she had ever heard.

"Hello you're married or did you forget?"

"Cami like I told you earlier, I'm only married on paper. Me and Louise are not your typical married couple. I'm just there for my kids because I know that if I left they would be fucked up. I've never loved anyone including my wife the way that I love you. I just need you to give some time to figure this all out. I don't want to hurt you and I definitely don't want to hurt my kids so I'm trying to do what's right for everyone involved."

When You Love Somebody

"I know you're trying to do the right thing Matt but I can't sell myself short hoping and praying that you'll leave your wife for me. Besides I don't want to be responsible for that kind of karma coming back to bite me." Cami got up to take her plate to the sink and Matt was right behind her. He pinned her to the sink with his groin and began to stroke the side of her face.

"Cami I love you and you love me. I'm not going anywhere and neither are you. I just need you to hold me down while I make some decisions. I don't want to do anything to hurt my kids or upset their lifestyle but on the other hand I know I can't keep living like this."

"That's my point neither can I"

Cami eased past Matt and walked into the living room all the while praying for God to give her the strength to be near Matt and not want to touch him or hug him.

"Listen, I know you deserve better than what I'm able to give you right now but I promise it won't always be that way. I give you my

LatimaNicole

word that I'm gonna figure this out and
soon."

When You Love Somebody

Chapter 10

Matt

It was 5:30 in the morning and Matt was sitting in front of the Queensboro Correctional Facility waiting for his father to be released. He had mixed emotions about seeing him. They hadn't actually seen each other in about 15 years and only started speaking after his mother died. In fact, Matt hadn't fully come to terms with the fact that he wasn't there for most of his life. Now that he had kids of his own he realized that parents weren't perfect and his were so far from it that it wasn't even funny. Queensboro wasn't your typical prison. There were no barbed wires or electronic gates surrounding the facility. The prison was housed in a nondescript building in an industrial area of Long Island City Queens. The facility served as transitional housing for inmates nearing the end of their sentences. Some were assigned to work release programs and others were there awaiting their release dates. Matt saw his father walk out of the door with a little duffle bag on his shoulder. He immediately recognized him because he could pass for his twin.

Bill "Dollar Bill" Cortlandt used to be the man back in the day but all of that hustling caught up to him and he wound up strung out on crack and getting arrested. When he was arrested he had two kilograms of cocaine on him and under New York State's RICO laws he was sentenced to a mandatory 15 years in prison. To this day he swore he and his crew were set up by a snitch. Bill looked up and down the block trying to locate Matt's white Navigator. Matt got out of the truck and called him over.

"Ayo Pops."

Bill quickened his steps and grinned from ear to ear.

"Hey young blood it's good to see you man. Thanks for coming to pick me up I really appreciate it. This is a smooth ride boy but

When You Love Somebody

it's big as hell. How much you spending in gas on this thing?"

"Trust me you don't want to know. I don't drive it much it's the family car."

"Back in the day if you wanted a family car you bought a station wagon or a minivan."

"Station wagon? Aww man that's too funny."

"Speaking of family, how's my grandbabies?"

"Everybody's good, kids getting big and grown. How are you Pop? How does it feel to finally touch down?"

"I don't know yet. I know I want to take a bath and eat some good food."

"Don't worry I got you covered. You wanna stop by the diner and get something to eat before we head to the crib?"

"Sounds good to me. I gotta check in with my parole officer at two."

"No doubt we'll get a quick bite and be out."

Matt drove over to the Georgia diner on Queens Boulevard and he could tell his Pops was a bit overwhelmed by how everything

LatimaNicole

had changed over the years. The waitress
seated them and gave them their menus.
Bill took forever to order. Everything on the
menu must have looked good to him.
Finally he settled on grits, eggs, salmon
croquettes and pancakes. He ate his food so
fast Matt didn't think he chewed it first.
Honestly, Matt thought, it felt good to be
there with him. This was something he
wished for when he was little. Most of the
time when Bill came around it was at night
when Matt was supposed to be sleeping. He
could hear his mother and father having sex
and always hoped that they would get back
together. But when they were finished his
Pops always made an excuse about why he
had to leave. His mother would get upset
and start crying or they would start arguing
and Matt's hopes of being a family went
right out the door with his father. He could
see the change in his father though. Prison
had a way of sucking the life out of a man.
He had an air of institutionalization about
him and Matt could tell he was looking to

When You Love Somebody

him to tell him what their next move would be.

"You ready Pop? I gotta get the kids ready for school."

"Yeah man I got the itis like a motherfucker. I could use a nice hot bath and a nap before I go see my PO."

"Okay that's cool. Let me get the check and we'll bounce."

When Matt pulled up to the house his father's eyes damn near popped out of his head.

"Boy you live in this neighborhood? You must be living large huh?"

"A lil sum sum."

Matt lived in a neighborhood called Hollis Hills. Hillside Avenue divided the neighborhood and to the south were modest one and two family homes. To the north where he lived, were the more palatial mini mansions. Matt pulled his truck into the driveway and clicked the remote to open the three car garage.

LatimaNicole

"Boy I thought I was living large in my day with my little condo by the water in Whitestone, but gotdamn that music must be paying off for you huh?"

"I do alright. I got my hands in a couple of investments, manage a couple of artists plus the producing thing."

"I'm proud of you son. I know I won't win no father of the year awards with you but I just want you to know you and your mother were my world. But between Nam and the streets my head was all fucked up. I knew I couldn't be the man your mother deserved so I stayed away most of the time. Cat was a special lady and I used to question myself all the time about what she saw in me. Truthfully she was way outta my league but me being a man and being selfish and greedy I couldn't let her go, and look because of me she's not here today."

"Pop for a long time I blamed you for my mom's death but she was a smart woman and she made her own choices. I've come to

When You Love Somebody

terms with it and made my peace with you and you should do the same."

"I guess you're right. Enough of that. I wanna meet my grandbabies."

They entered the house through the garage and walked into the kitchen. Matt didn't have to get the kids up until 7:30 so he sat at the kitchen counter and watched his father. Bill was standing up against the wall taking everything in. He guessed his dad was kind of nervous and was trying not to show it so he decided to give him a break.

"Have a seat Pop. What you standing up against the wall for? Ain't nobody gonna bite you."

"You funny boy. I ain't worried about nobody biting me. Just trying to get my bearings that's all. I like the way you got everything laid out here. It's real nice."

"Well how about we see the rest of the house then. I'll show you around and then you can take your stuff up to your room and relax. I gave you the upstairs guest room because it has the biggest bathroom and a little mini fridge."

"Man you forgot I'm coming from a 6x8' cell with a toilet that doubled as a sink and a shower. Anything you put me up in would be an improvement."

"I know Pop but I want to make sure you are comfortable and I have a feeling you won't be in that room by yourself for long."

"What you mean?"

"As soon as them rugrats know you're here they are gonna take over I bet you."

"Well in that case, give me the big room so my babies can hang out with me."

Matt couldn't help but grin. His dad was always getting on him about spoiling the kids but something told him he was gonna eat his words.

"Pop everything you need is right there in the linen closet next to the tub. Go ahead, take your bath and relax. I'll wake you up when it's time for you to go check in."

"Thanks youngblood. I really appreciate everything. Especially since you coulda

When You Love Somebody

kicked me to the curb and there wouldn't have been a damn thing I could say about it."

"I could never do that Pop. Then I wouldn't ever have any luck. Like I said the past is the past. Now if you start showing your ass you better believe you gonna be kicked to the curb so fast you'll have skid marks on your butt."

"I hear that youngblood."

Chapter 11

Camille

"Damn Keish you look like you're ready to pop."

"Cami I can't wait to have this baby I feel like a stuffed sausage."

"You look beautiful though. Your skin is glowing and your hair is growing all over the place not to mention how big your boobs are. I know Paul is loving it."

"Paul is in seventh heaven girl. He's been so attentive and sweet this entire pregnancy. He's more excited than I am."

"I'm glad to see he's finally getting his shit together it's been a long time coming."

Keisha sat back in her chair and rubbed her stomach.

"Aww man this baby can kick. I might have a little football player in here."

"You don't know what you're having? I would have thought you would have wanted to find out."

When You Love Somebody

"Nope I want it to be a surprise. Of course Paul is hoping for a boy he keeps saying my little man this and my little man that."

"I'm so happy for you Keish since we were little that's all you've ever talked about was having a baby."

Camille got up and hugged Keisha.

"I can't wait until your shower I already got your gift.'

"Now don't think you're gonna just be buying up everything and spoiling this baby to death because it's not gonna happen."

"You can't tell me what to do with my money, if I want to spend it all in the baby section that's my business."

"Ok well do you. I'm going to pick up my God babies and spend some time with them. I'll talk to you later."

Keisha waddled out of the restaurant to her car as Cami stayed behind lost in thought. She unconsciously rubbed her belly as she thought about how it would feel to have Matt's baby growing inside of her. Realizing that she needed to get a serious grip on reality, she quickly scanned the restaurant to see if anyone was looking at her and high tailed it out of there.

Keisha pulled up to Matt's house, got out of the car and rang the bell. Louise came to the door with her face frowned up. "The kids will be ready in a minute" she said while walking into the house and leaving the door open, not even bothering to invite Keisha in.

"Hello to you too Louise." Keisha hoped that she could just pick up the kids and be on her way. She wasn't in the mood for any drama and knowing Louise anything was possible. The kids came running through the door yelling "Auntie Keisha Auntie Keisha", racing to be the first to give her a hug.

"Go get in the car ya'll. MJ make you sure you buckle your sister in the car seat." Louise shooed the kids away while putting her hand up to Keisha as if to tell her to wait.

When You Love Somebody

"Keisha I wanna ask you a question and I need you to keep it one hundred with me."

Oh boy here we go. She knew it was too good to be true

"What's up Louise?"

"I'm just gonna come right out with it. Ain't no need to beat around the bush. Is Matt fucking around with somebody?"

"How would I know? I hardly ever see Matt and when I do he's usually with Paul or the kids."

"Look Keisha I know we ain't friends and you don't owe me nothing but I'm sure you and Paul be doing that pillow talking shit and he might have mentioned something to you."

"Louise where is this coming from? Paul hasn't mentioned anything to me about Matt cheating and frankly if he was I don't want to know about it. Honestly I can't see Matt doing nothing like that. Now Paul on the other hand, that's a different story. But what makes you think he's cheating?"

LatimaNicole

"A woman knows these things. I ain't stupid. He walking around here all happy and shit like he won the fucking lottery and been asking you to babysit the kids. I know something is going on I just can't put my finger on it."

"If I had to guess maybe he's just working hard, your lifestyle isn't cheap you know." Keisha had to remind her that she was blessed for someone that didn't lift a finger to take care of herself or her kids.

"Louise I gotta go but if I was you I wouldn't worry about Matt. His family is the most important thing to him."

"Yeah you're right I'm probably just tripping."

As Keisha drove home she couldn't help thinking about what Louise had said. She felt bad for lying and even worse because her own flesh and blood was the other woman. As many times as Paul had cheated on her she knew exactly how it felt to find out the person you vowed to spend the rest of your life with had gone outside the

When You Love Somebody

marriage and had relations with another woman. On the other hand, from the outside looking in, she didn't see where Matt and Louise's marriage was built on love. It seemed to be more of a business arrangement than anything else.

Keisha was so deep in thought that she didn't see the green Honda Accord run the light. Before she knew it the car had slammed into her passenger side and sent the car spinning across the intersection. When she woke up she was in the hospital with tubes in her nose an IV in her right arm and a cast on her left arm. Paul was at her bedside and he looked as if he'd been crying. She tried to speak but her voice was so dry Paul's name came out in a scratchy whisper. As she closed her eyes the accident started to come back to her in bits and pieces. She felt her stomach and it was flat as a board. In her head she screamed no as she drifted back off to sleep.

LatimaNicole

This was the third time Matt was a getting a call from Paul. The first two times he let the calls go to voicemail as he pleaded with Cami to give him some time to figure their situation out.

"Something must be wrong. Paul wouldn't blow up my phone like this unless something was wrong. Let me take this call baby." He pressed the answer call button on his phone.

"Yo P what up?"

"Yo man Keisha and the kids were in a car accident."

"What!!!!! Are they ok? Where are they? I'm on my way."

Cami started to panic from the tone in Matt's voice.

"Matt what happened?"

"Kiesha and the kids were in an accident." Matt said rubbing his head.

"What!" I screamed. "Where? When? Where are they now?"

"They're at Northshore get your coat come on we gotta go."

When You Love Somebody

Matt was driving like a bat out of hell and Cami was holding on to the oh shit bar so hard that her knuckles were turning white. How could this have happened? She was so scared that they were going to hear awful news when they got to the hospital. Paul didn't give Matt any information and her mind feared the worse. They made it to the hospital in record time and ran straight to the emergency reception area.

"Hi my name is Matthew Cortlandt I'm looking for my children. They were brought in for a car accident."

"And I'm looking for Keisha Simpson she was involved in the same accident."

The nurse looked in the computer and shook her head. "I'm sorry but I can't give you any information on Mrs. Simpson unless you're her next of kin. Sir if you have a seat in the waiting area the Doctor will be out to speak to you soon."

What did she mean next of kin? Did Keisha die? OH MY GOD please let Keisha and the baby be okay. She couldn't take another death. Matt grabbed her and steered her toward the reception area. Paul was sitting there with his head in his hands and it looked as if he'd been crying. She ran over to Paul and immediately started asking questions.

"Paul what's going on? Where's Keisha? How's the baby and the kids?"

"The kids are fine they got a few bumps and bruises and MJ broke his arm but other than that they're okay. Keisha suffered a concussion and a broken jaw from the airbag and she fractured her wrist."

"What about the baby?"

"They delivered the baby. It's a boy 7lbs 6oz. He's a fighter and he is doing good."

"Oh Thank God. I was so worried. When can I see her? Where is she?"

"They're transferring her to a room now that's why I'm sitting out here. The kids are in the pediatric emergency room Matt. I checked on them already but I know they'll be happy to see you."

When You Love Somebody

Matt started walking in the direction that Paul had pointed to when a petite brown skinned woman with an unnecessarily long weave, fake eyelashes and bright red fingernails walked in to the waiting area and fell into Matt's arms sobbing.

"Oh Matt what happened? Where are our babies? Are they okay? I rushed over here as soon as Paul called me."

Matt looked at Cami and mouthed "I'm sorry" as he led Louise away from the waiting room.

Cami sank down in a chair as the realization that she'd just came face to face with Matt's wife smacked her upside her head. Of course she knew he was married but just didn't think about it. He never brought her into their world and she was grateful for that. But seeing her in the flesh gave Cami a harsh reality check. She was in love with a married man. She was in LOVE with a married man. How could she let this happen? How did he get past the wall she put up in every other relationship she'd ever

LatimaNicole

had. Matt had always been so tender and patient with her and he didn't fall for her tough exterior, in fact he saw right through it. He knew all about her abandonment issues and did everything to reassure her that he wasn't going anywhere. Shit why should he? He had the best of both worlds. It was her that had to put an end to this. Her rational, analytical side knew that she'd have to end it but a part of her didn't want to lose Matt. If he didn't have all of that baggage he would be the perfect guy for her. Their relationship was based on genuine respect and communication. They talked about any and everything. Sometimes he'd call in the middle of the day to tell a funny story or she'd call him to vent about her clients. There was a real friendship there that she didn't want to lose. But she knew they couldn't be just friends, there were too many emotions involved. She was gonna have to remove Matt from her life completely.

When You Love Somebody

The nurse snapped Cami out of her thoughts when she announced that Keisha had been moved to her room and could have visitors for a little while. She and Paul took the elevator up to the Labor and Delivery floor of the hospital each lost in their own thoughts. When they got to the room, Paul told Cami to go in first. The sight of Keisha with all those tubes and bandages made Cami want to run in the opposite direction but she knew she had to be strong for her sister cousin.

"Hey baby girl how are you feeling?" She asked Keisha as she rubbed her hair.

"I'm in a lot of pain. My face is killing me and they stapled me after the C-section. But I'm grateful to be alive and to have a healthy baby. Can you believe it I'm a mom?"

"I know. I'm so happy for you and Paul. Especially you, you deserve to be happy. Paul is walking around like Big Daddy. You can't tell him nothing."

LatimaNicole

"You know my baby shower is Saturday. They better let me out before then. I need to get myself together."

"Girl don't you worry about that. I've got everything under control all I need you to do is get better so you can take care of my Godson."

"I'm fine. Just sore. I'm trying to get the doctor to discharge me by tomorrow."

"Tomorrow? Are you crazy? You just got here. What do you mean tomorrow? You need to chill out and get some rest. You know once you get that baby home there won't be any resting for you."

"You know I never liked hospitals Cami. Besides how can I rest when the nurses are in here every hour poking and prodding me like I'm a damn guinea pig?"

"I know that's why I'm not gonna stay long. I have a lot of running around to do but if you need something just call me ok."

"I'm fine and I know my husband is somewhere within spitting distance so I'll just put him to work. Before you go though,

When You Love Somebody

Paul told me that you saw Louise. How do you feel about that?"

"Honestly, I've been so worried about you, PJ and the kids that I haven't had a chance to process anything. But I can't lie, I felt like shit as they were walking away to go check on the kids. Regardless of what Matt says about his home life, seeing them two together really hit home."

"So what are you gonna do?"

"I don't know Keish. I think I'm in too deep. But I do know I have to have a talk with Matt. We have some decisions to make. I be damn if I spend my life being somebody's mistress. But you wanna know what's crazy? He's never made me feel as if I'm the other woman. I feel so secure with him that I'm starting to think about a future with him."

"Wow! You got it bad girl."

"I know and a part of me says I should just ride it 'til the wheels fall off but the other part of me knows that I deserve to be with a

man that can give me one hundred percent.
I'll see you later sister cousin get some rest."

"I'll try."

As soon as she got in her car Cami called
Matt. She wanted to check on the kids but
also wanted to see him so they could talk.
Her heart kept telling her that Matt was the
man for her but her brain still had that wall
up to protect her from getting hurt.

"Hey Babe how you doing?"

"I'm good Matt. I just left the hospital and
was wondering if I could I see you tonight?"

"Of course you can. I have some things to
wrap up in the studio with Rasheed but I can
always end the session early. What's on
your mind? You sound like you stressing
about something."

"Yeah, kinda sorta. I've been thinking
about us a lot and we need to talk about
where this is going."

"Cami we've had this conversation before
you know I'm not going anywhere so I don't
know why you stressing."

When You Love Somebody

"I'm just not comfortable doing number two. I deserve more. As much as I love you, I love myself more and I have to do the right thing."

"I don't want to talk about this anymore I'll see you tonight."

And with that Matt hung up the phone. Cami thought, "What the hell did she get herself into"? Matt wasn't taking no for an answer and she wasn't strong enough to really put her foot down. She was hoping that he would agree with her and let her off the hook but there was a slim chance in hell of him agreeing to break it off. She had a feeling that no matter what happened between her and Matt she would let him back in her life whenever he needed her.

Cami had been running around all week trying to get everything she needed for Keisha's baby shower that she hardly had time for Matt which was fine with her. The last time they saw each other nothing was resolved and all they wound up doing was

what they always did, make love and spend
the night wrapped in each other's arms.
Cami believed that she didn't end it with
Matt because deep down inside she didn't
want to. He was the man of her dreams. He
was everything she had hoped and prayed
for. He put her on a pedestal and made her
feel special, like she mattered to him. He
discussed things with her about the kids,
about his music and about decisions he
needed to make and she did the same. If
something happened in his life good or bad
she was the first person he shared the news
with. He did little things to let her know he
was thinking about her like sending little
gifts to her at work or texting her in the
middle of the day with corny quotes to make
her laugh. He was gentle and understanding
of her flaws and let her know every day that
he wasn't going anywhere which was her
biggest fear. He knew she had attachment
issues and did everything he could to
reassure her that he wouldn't hurt or
abandon her. Cami tried not to acknowledge

When You Love Somebody

the pink elephant in the room because it was
the one thing that kept her up at night and
also kept her from having the proverbial
perfect relationship.

Chapter 12

Matt

They baby shower was so much fun. Little PJ looked fly sitting in his prince's chair. Kiesha and Paul were so happy. They got so many gifts that Paul had to make three trips in his truck to get everything home. After the shower Matt and Cami went to an event for a new brand of liquor that one of his friends was launching. The event was a typical industry function with the who's who of music jockeying to be noticed. Cami didn't like to attend those types of events because she thought they were phony. Matt had to convince her that it would be a great chance to network and make contacts. Cami argued that most of the people in the industry lacked integrity and when they gave out their contact information they never followed up. Their favorite expression was "I got you," which really meant "I have no intentions on contacting you but I'll take your number anyway." Cami didn't really

When You Love Somebody

want to be bothered, she rarely went to those
types of things unless she was working but
Matt practically begged her and she agreed
even though she had a bad feeling about
being out in public with him so openly. Matt
was so busy showing Cami off, he didn't
even notice that Louise's friend Danielle
was at the party and had taken a photo of
them and sent it to Louise.

When Matt got home the next
morning Louise was all over him.
"Where the fuck you been Matt?"
"Who you talking to like that Louise? Since
when you start questioning me about where
I been?"
"I got a better question for you. Who the
fuck is this bitch and why is she all up in
your fucking face?"
Matt took the phone from Louise and his
heart caught in his throat when he saw the
picture of him and Cami sitting at a table
appearing to be in their own little world. It
looked as if he was kissing Cami on the
cheek but in reality he was whispering in her

ear what he was going to do to her when he got her home.

"Louise chill out you making a big deal out of nothing. That's Keisha's cousin the one that took the family portrait of me and the kids."

"You fucking her? Cause you damn sure ain't been fucking me."

"Louise ain't nobody got time for your bullshit. I gotta get the kids ready for school."

"Don't be tryna play me Matt cause trust and believe I got something for that ass."

"What you gonna do huh? Get pregnant again?

Louise's jaw dropped when Matt said that.

"Yeah I heard you and your home girl on the phone you ain't slick. Why you think I haven't been fucking around with you. You trifling and always have been. So before you start accusing me of fucking around you better make sure your shit is straight. Now I'm going to get the kids ready for school"

When You Love Somebody

How could he have been so careless? Matt thought to himself. He was getting comfortable with the situation with Cami and was starting to act like Paul. He never meant for what he did out in the street to hit home but even though Louise was his wife, Cami was his woman and secretly he wanted everybody to know it. Good thing he was able to shut Louise down before she got all hype and tried to swing on him like she used to do back in the days.

"Sonny it's time to get up. Sonny come on lil man time to get ready for school." Matt shook Sonny and pulled the covers off of him trying to get him up. He just wasn't a morning person. Finally, Sonny opened one eye and scooted to the bottom of the bed.

"Dad can I stay home today?"

"Why? What's the matter? You don't feel well?"

'Nah, I feel fine but I wanna stay home and make sure Mom is ok she was crying last night."

LatimaNicole

Matt felt like shit. He never wanted to expose his kids to his infidelity. All this time he thought he was being careful but as his feelings for Cami grew stronger, he became more and more reckless.

"Did your Mom say what was wrong?"

"She said she was having a bad day."

"Ok well today is a new day and I'll talk to her and make sure she feels better. Cool?"

"Cool."

"Alright lil man get up and start getting ready then wake your sister up. I'm gonna go downstairs and start making breakfast."

"Ok Dad."

Matt walked in the kitchen and his father was sitting at the breakfast bar drinking coffee and reading the paper.

"Good morning youngblood."

"Morning Pop."

"Just getting in huh?"

"Yeah man I had an event to go to last night."

"What kind of partying ya'll doing now a days where you don't get home til seven in

When You Love Somebody

the morning? Back in my day if you went out partying you didn't let the sunlight beat you home unless you got lucky and hooked up with a lil tenderoni."

"Nah Pop I ain't tryna mess with these industry broads they ain't looking for nothing but a come up."

"Now I ain't tryna get in ya business but that wife of yours wasn't too happy last night and something tells me it ain't cause you went out last night."

"It's a long story Pop why don't you ride with me to take the kids to school so we can talk."

"Sounds like a plan. Let me go see what them munchkins is up to up there."

Matt waited until he had dropped the kids off before he made his confession.

"I met somebody Pop."

"Shit boy you ain't got to tell me. You walking around here with your nose open wider than the Grand Canyon."

"Is it that obvious?"

LatimaNicole

"To me it is cause I'm a man and I've been there before. I used to be the same way with your mother. Man she had me sprung."

"Well I guess you can say I'm sprung too. I've never met a woman like her before Pop. She's everything I never knew I needed in a woman. I think I'm in love with her."

"So what you gonna do? You either got to shit or get off the pot son. The little bit I know about Louise, she ain't the type to take your word for face value. And I'm sure you know a woman's intuition is a motherfucker."

"Well she got more than her intuition. One of her trifling home girls sent her a picture of me and Cami at the party last night. That's why she was crying. To be honest though I'm surprised at her. I didn't think her selfish ass cared what I did as long as I took care of home and she didn't have to lift a finger to do shit."

"Now look a here young blood that's your wife and the mother of your children. You telling me there's no love lost between

When You Love Somebody

ya'll? If for nothing else you owe her respect for bringing them babies into this world."

"Don't get me wrong Pop. I care about Louise but I'm not in love with her. Never was. I only married her because she got pregnant. Back then I wasn't looking for love, shit I didn't even want no kids."

"So what you telling me she trapped you?"

"In a way yeah. She knew what it was and she chose to have the baby anyway. I always said if I ever had kids I wasn't gonna walk out on them like you did me and she knew that and ran with it."

"So if you didn't want no kids why didn't you strap up boy?"

"I did. After Mya was born I found out that she put a hole in the condom and got pregnant with Sonny on purpose. By that time we was two kids in and she flipped the script on me. She started hanging out and shopping all the time and not taking care of the house. So I did what I had to do to make sure my kids were good. I know Louise got her shit with her but I don't want to see her hurt. She held me down in the beginning when I was first starting out so I kind of understand why she is the way she is. I guess she figures it's her turn now. But Pops Cami is different she ain't on no tit for tat shit. She's on her grind taking her career to the next level and I know she's with me because she wants to be not because she gotta to be."

"Well youngin I'ma tell you something, it don't make no sense in you trying to hold something together that's broke cause as soon as you let go it's gonna fall to pieces anyway. Now as for them babies, they smarter than you think they are and they can tell when something ain't right. You gonna do more harm to them by pretending. It's best ya'll be honest with them kids and show them what a real relationship is supposed to look like cause your marriage ain't it."

"I know Pops. I know."

When You Love Somebody

Chapter 13
Camille

Cami went over to Keisha's to spend some time with her and the baby. She was so happy for Keisha and holding little PJ in her arms made her heart twinge with a tiny bit of jealousy. Ever since Keisha had PJ Cami felt her biological clock ticking like a time bomb and she longed to have a baby of her own.

"Paul and I are going to renew our vows."

"Oh Keisha that's great. Did you set a date yet?"

"Yeah we're thinking about the end of September. PJ will be six months by then and it's gonna take me about that long to get rid of this baby gut."

"Girl please you hardly look like you had a baby."

"That's because I've been wearing this damn girdle like granny taught us. But anyway I wanted to know would you be my maid of honor?"

LatimaNicole

"Hell yeah! You better not ask anyone else. I guess that means Matt is gonna be Paul's best man."

"Of course."

Cami tried to cover her frown but Keisha caught on.

"How are you and Matt doing these days?"

"I don't know. One week I'm madly in love with him and wish I could spend the rest of my life with him and the next I'm trying to break it off and get him out of my system but he won't let go. He keeps saying he's gonna work it out but I can't afford to sit around and wait for him to decide what he's gonna do."

"I hear you. I wouldn't want to be in your shoes. I wanna ask you a question though. How do you feel being the other woman? Are you becoming comfortable with that role? I mean as a married woman a part of me feels like what you're doing is fucked up. You know I've been on the other side more times than I can count and that's just the times I know about. I feel that we as

When You Love Somebody

women should respect each other's relationships. Men and women go through their ups and downs but us women make it too easy for men to not have to put the work in because they know they can always run to the next one."

"That's so true but Keish you know me. You know I would never have set out to be with Matt on purpose. Shit look how hard I've been on Paul over the years. I'm not condoning my relationship with Matt. I know it's wrong but my heart is all in and as hard as I try I can't seem to let go."

"Has he ever said he was unhappy at home?"

"For the most part he tries not to involve me with what goes on in his home but one time he was feeling a bit emotional I guess and he poured his heart out. He said he had a conversation with his Dad and he realized that his home life was affecting the kids. He told me when we first started seeing each other that he was never really in love with his wife and he only married her because she got pregnant and then she kept getting pregnant and he wanted to be there for his kids."

"And you believe that?"

"I have no reason not to. He said the first time she got pregnant she put a hole in the condom. He also said that he was never in a real relationship with her. She was just someone he used when he was in the streets hustling. It sounds foul but he only had sex with her to keep her loyal."

"What happened to the Cami I know? I've known Matt for a long time and he never struck me as a liar but I've known you all my life and if any other dude would have hit you with that line you would have ran for the hills."

"I know isn't that crazy? My head knows everything you're saying is truth but my heart has a mind of its' own,"

"Girl you got it bad. I pray everything works out one way or another. You don't deserve to be in limbo like this."

When You Love Somebody

"That's just it. I don't feel like I'm in limbo at all. There's never been a time where I needed Matt and he wasn't there for me. Sure I wish I could spend more time with him but that's only because of our schedules it has nothing to do with his home life,"

"I'm praying for you sister-cousin. I don't want to see you hurt. It took you a long time to get over Hassan and you don't deserve to go through that again."

"Tell me about it. All I can do is keep the faith and hope that everything works out for the best. Can we talk about something else now? How bout this vow renewal?"

"Well it won't be anything big. I was thinking something really intimate at the restaurant with you, Matt and the kids as the wedding party and then a few friends and family."

"You need me to do anything? I'm at your beck and call."

"Can you go with me to pick out a dress? I have a wedding planner handling all of the other details and the chef from the restaurant is going to make all of the food."

"OK when do you want to go? My week is kind of light except for class on Tuesday and Thursday."

"How about Friday morning? I can get Paul to stay with PJ and we can make a day of it."

"That sounds cool. So I'm gonna be the Maid of Honor and Matt is gonna be the Best Man?"

"Yup."

Cami looked at the smirk on Keisha's face and said, "You don't have to look so thrilled."

"Ha. It will be one big happy family. You, Matt and your step children will look so handsome in the wedding pictures."

Cami grabbed the sofa cushion and hurled it at Keisha. "Screw you heifer! I'm glad you find this so damn funny."

"You know I gotta mess with you girl. I haven't seen you in ages. Your man got you on lock down so you act like you don't know nobody."

When You Love Somebody

"Whatever fat ass. That's why they're gonna have to sew two dresses together to fit all that junk you got in your trunk."

"I know you aint talking Ms. Bootylicious, all that ass and hips you dragging around."

"Green is not your color honey. Don't be jealous."

Cami barely got to her car before her phone started ringing.

"Hello."

"Hey Babe what you doing?"

"Hey you. I just left Keisha's. I'm on my way to the studio to work on some proofs. Why? Wassup?"

"I wanna see you."

"That didn't sound too good what's wrong?"

"Somebody sent a picture of us to Louise and she was bugging out this morning but I handled it."

"What do you mean you handled it? Oh my God what are we going to do? I don't think it's a good idea for us to see each other Matt. Your wife has a picture of me, she knows what I look like. This is not good."

LatimaNicole

"Calm down Cami. I said I handled it. You have nothing to worry about. And what you mean it's not a good idea for us to see each other? Don't play with me Cami. I'll be at your studio in 30 minutes."

Matt must have been out of his mind, Cami thought. She couldn't understand how he still wanted to see her as if nothing happened. Things were getting too crazy for her and when she saw Matt she was going to give him an ultimatum. He had to choose either her or his wife. She couldn't keep putting herself through this rollercoaster of a relationship. She just didn't know if she was strong enough to do what she needed to do. How could she let this happen? She questioned herself. She'd always prided herself on the fact that she had morals when it came to her dating life and for the most part she had stuck to her principles. But there was something about Matt that caused her to throw caution to the wind.

When You Love Somebody

As Matt drove over to Cami's studio he thought about his predicament. He knew for a fact he wasn't ready to let Cami go and he damn sure wasn't gonna leave his kids with Louise. He knew what he had to do. Cami just had to give him some time to put everything in place. He needed her just like he needed air to breathe. She was his partner, his confidant, his soul mate. He pulled up to Cami's studio and got out of the car. For some reason he hesitated before ringing the bell. He knew that Louise knowing how she looked didn't sit right with Cami. He had to convince her that he had everything under control. He rang the bell and Cami buzzed him up.

"Hey baby."

"What's up Matt?"

"Where you going? Where's my kiss?"

"I'm not in a kissing mood."

"Cami look at me." Matt took his index finger and lifted her chin up to reach his lips but kissed her on the forehead instead. He grabbed her in an embrace and held her for what to Cami seemed like forever.

"Matt let me go."

"No Cami I can't let you go. I won't let you go."

"What do you mean you won't let me go? Are you serious?"

"I'm serious as cancer."

Cami tried to break free but Matt just held her tighter until finally she gave up and sunk into his embrace. She didn't understand why she always felt so safe in his arms. Even with everything that was going on with his wife seeing a picture of them together, she still felt like he would protect her at all costs. She didn't want to love Matt but she did. She didn't want to share the only man that had managed to break down the wall she had built around her heart but she was. This was her reality and as mighty and self-righteous as she could be at times, there was a force holding her in this moment, in this space, in Matt's arms. Resistance was damn near impossible. But she had to be strong.

When You Love Somebody

She was familiar with strong. It's what she had to be all of her life. When her parents died everyone told her to be strong when all she wanted to do was crawl in her daddy's lap like she used to. When she had to work her way through college, everyone said, "you're strong you can do it." When her grandmother died in her senior year of college, her family said "Cami will take care of everything she's built for stuff like this," and they looked to her to make the arrangements and settle her grandmother's affairs.

Truth was Cami was tired. She was tired of being strong. She wanted for once in her life to be vulnerable and know that she wouldn't be taken advantage of. To be soft and mushy and emotional, but most of all Cami wanted to feel safe. For some odd reason, she found that sense of security in Matt. Even though she knew that their relationship was morally wrong, she sometimes felt like she deserved to be a little selfish instead of always thinking about how her actions might affect

LatimaNicole

others. For once she wanted to be taken care of and not the caretaker.

"Cami besides my kids, you are the best thing to ever happen to me. I am not letting you walk out of my life. You can't and you won't."

"Matt I need some time with this. I don't need nor am I looking for any drama. I'm a woman so I know how we women think. You think it's handled but I'm telling you it's just the beginning. Once a woman gets suspicious she won't stop until she finds what she's looking for."

"Don't you understand? I don't care! She can do all the snooping she wants, as long as she doesn't step to you or try to get my kids involved we good. I don't want her, I want you Cami."

"You say that now Matt but when the accusations start flying and she's going through your phone and showing up where she knows you're going to be or following you, you're going to change your tune. I just can't risk it."

When You Love Somebody

"All I'm asking is for you to give me some time. You're my woman. You're supposed to believe in me. I've never lied to you Cami. Never. I've always been 100 with you about everything. Shit I've told you things about me that I never told a soul. In a perfect world you would be my wife and the mother of my children. But there's no such thing as perfect is there? I need you. I need you more than I want to admit."

Cami balled up her fists and pounded Matt's chest in an attempt to free herself from his embrace. She needed some space to think, to breathe. His Yves Saint Laurent cologne was intoxicating and the longer she stayed wrapped in his arms the harder it was for her to come up with a convincing argument as to why this relationship in its current state would never work. Matt released Cami and sat down in a chair with his face in his hands. He sat in that position for what seemed like forever. Not moving, not looking up at Cami. Truth be told he was scared to look at her. He was afraid of what he might see in her eyes. He couldn't bear to see Cami hurt or even worse, the look of a woman who had had enough.

"Matt look at me."

Matt raised his head slowly and looked in her direction.

"Look at me."

He focused on her face but refused to look her in the eye.

Cami knelt down on the floor in front of him and put his face in her hands.

"You know I love you right?"

"Yes Cami I know."

"Do you love me?"

"Yes."

"Would you ever do anything to intentionally hurt me?"

"Hell no."

"So I'm going to trust you when you say that you're going to work this out. But I don't want you to think that I'm okay with this situation because I'm not. You have to figure this out and soon."

"I know baby. I know."

When You Love Somebody

Matt kissed Cami's hands, her arms and finally worked his way up to her neck. Cami pulled away, got up and walked out of the room. Matt sat there stunned for a minute and then went after her. He caught up with her and pinned her against the wall.

"Don't walk away from me Cami."

Cami said nothing as she stared in his eyes. The look of pleading and earnestness was enough to make her heart melt. Matt picked her up and wrapped her legs around his waist while he snuggled his nose in the crease of her breast. Cami grabbed the back of his head and pushed it further into her breast. Matt carried her to the reception area and laid her on the couch. Slowly he undressed her and then himself. He picked Cami up again and hoisted her up so that her legs were wrapped around his shoulders then he pinned her to the wall. With slow deliberate strokes, he invaded Cami's already moist vagina with his tongue. Next he flattened his tongue and licked her clit until Cami started to writhe with pleasure.

LatimaNicole

He dropped her down to his waist, entered
her and Cami gasped. He made love to her
with gentle calculated strokes, teasing the
entrance to her womanhood with the tip of
his penis. Cami could barely contain herself
but she wanted to hold on to the feeling for
as long as she could. She felt the buildup as
her vaginal muscles began to tighten. Not
being able to hold back anymore she rocked
back and forth while Matt palmed her butt
cheeks. Neither of them said a word. Cami
exploded first and then Matt pulled out and
released his milk onto Cami's stomach.
Matt let her down and steered her to the
couch. He went into the bathroom, got some
paper towels, soaped them up and came
back and wiped Cami down. He laid next to
her staring into her eyes and stroking her
hair until he fell asleep. Cami was so
satiated that she couldn't move. Her legs felt
like rubber and she could feel her heart
beating through her chest. She watched Matt
as he slept thinking to herself that if she
could, she would stay in this exact moment

When You Love Somebody

forever. She was never the type to keep a man around just for the sake of having a man but she had to admit that she was slowly beginning to accept the fact that this was her reality. She would rather deal with Matt and his baggage than not have a chance at having him in her life.

She put her hand to her forehead as the realization of what she was thinking set in. She was willing to be the mistress just to keep this man in her life.

Chapter 13

The Wedding

"Are you ready to do this Keish?" Cami beamed at her sister cousin.

"As ready as I'll ever be. I just want to say thank you for all of your help putting this together. I couldn't have done any of it without you."

"Girl please. It was my pleasure. At least one of us will get the fairytale wedding we always talked about."

"Don't talk like that Cami, your day is coming. I see the way Matt looks at you, you got his nose open."

"Don't even bring his name up. Its' bad enough we're gonna be joined at the hip all day. I've been trying to keep him at a distance ever since his wife saw those pictures. But it's hard. I finally had to admit to myself that I really love that man and there is nothing I can do about it."

"You can't control who you fall in love with Cami. You either choose to accept it and try

When You Love Somebody

to build a relationship with that person or you move on."

"That's the thing. I've talked myself to death about me and Matt. I've weighed the pros and cons of this relationship. You know me I analyze everything. But I keep coming back to how he makes me feel. I've never had a man who gets me like Matt does. Am I being selfish Keish? Like really, the man I love is married. Regardless of what he does or doesn't do, he goes home to another woman. Am I settling?"

"You know I don't condone cheating and technically Matt is a cheater and you are his chick on the side. That's the reality of your situation but I know you and I know Matt and I've never seen two people who belong together more than the two of you."

"So what am I supposed to do?"

"I can't tell you what to do. You have to figure that out on your own. But enough about you and Matt this is supposed to be my day now help me with my dress."

LatimaNicole

"I'm so sorry you're right. By the way you look beautiful, you're glowing."

"I'm in a good place right now. Paul and I are in a good place; after all these years I think he finally gets it."

A knock on the door broke up the ladies conversation.

"Who is it?" Keisha yelled through the door.

"It's your mother-in-law can I come in?"

"Yes. Please come in Mrs. Williams."

Paul's mother walked in the room and drew in her breath.

"Oh Keisha you look stunning. My son is a lucky man."

"Thank you Mrs. Williams."

"No thank you. If it wasn't for you I don't know where that boy would be. You stuck by his side through all the foolishness and carrying on he did. Believe me I knew what was going on but what was I supposed to do? He's my son and as much as I love you I felt I needed to just mind my business and pray he would get his act together."

When You Love Somebody

"You don't know how much that means to me. I always thought to myself, how could you being a woman, not feel some type of way about the things that Paul was doing."

"Girl, I used to get on Junior all the time. I warned him that if he kept it up he was going to lose you. But I guess the apple don't fall far from the tree. Junior's father was a SOB and I guess I should have done a better job of shielding him from all the mess I went through with Paul Sr. and his cheating behind. But enough of that this is your day and all that mess is in the past. We need to focus on the future."

She then reached in and gave Keisha a hug and said, "I love you Keisha. You're the daughter I never had."

After they all wiped their tears and the make-up artist re-applied their make-up it was time to get the show on the road.

Paul was pacing back and forth across the floor of the hotel suite. For some strange reason he was nervous. He woke up not only hung over from the bachelor party but also with the feeling that the wedding wasn't going to go as smooth as planned. In the back of his mind he kept telling himself it would serve him right if Keisha just took the baby and bounced and left him standing at the altar.

"Yo P man you gonna wear a hole in that carpet if you keep pacing back and forth. Chill out man. I don't know why you so nervous, you're just renewing your vows."

"I know Matt but I got a bad vibe man. I don't know what it is but something ain't right."

"I know what it is. It's all that Cristal you drank last night. You probably still drunk."

"I'm good man. But yo what's this I hear you got a special surprise for me and Keisha?"

"It's really a surprise for Keisha. Me and Rasheed worked on a lil something in the studio and he's gonna perform it for ya'll first dance."

"Oh word? That's what's up. What made you come up with that?"

When You Love Somebody

"On some real shit, I wrote it thinking about Cami."

"Shorty got you open huh boy?"

"Something like that. Man Cami is special. She's not like these chicks out here who be with a nigga for what he can do for them. She got her own thing going on and she don't be sweating me. What's bugged out is how we never linked up before. Nigga I been knowing you all my life and you and Keisha been together forever, how the hell I never met her is just crazy to me. I definitely would have bagged her."

"Nah man. We were on some other shit back in the days. You know you wasn't no looking for love type nigga back then. We was caught up in the game and she never was the type to fuck with a street nigga."

"Maybe you're right but I got her now. I think."

"Whatchu mean you think?"

"She been keeping her distance ever since I told her Wee saw a flick of me and her. She was never cool with the married thing and I guess the reality kinda set in."

"Yeah to tell you the truth I was shocked as hell that she even rocked with you for as long as she did. She never was the type to stay with a nigga if he aint doing right."

"Tell me about it. Even though she never was on some ra ra shit she definitely let me know she wasn't feeling the situation. But that's what I love about her. She so smooth with her shit. She'll let you know how she feel but as far as all that arguing and fighting shit she not the one for that. She be on some you better pay attention nigga because I'm not gonna repeat myself type shit."

"Ha that sounds just like her. But my nigga did you just say you love her?"

"What I said was that's what I love about her."

"Same difference. If you love her you love her sometimes we don't get to choose."

"Aint that the truth"

"Get the door man."

"Hey Pop what up?"

When You Love Somebody

"You cats ready to get this show on the road?"

"Yeah Mr. C, I can't wait to see my bride."

"Well young buck let's get moving then. It's show time!"

Matt, Paul and Mr. Chandler walked across the hall to the private banquet room and took their places. The smell of hundreds of calla lilies gently perfumed the air and Paul started to feel butterflies fluttering in his stomach. The music began and the sound of Mary J. Blige's "I Found My Everything" filled the room. Maya and Misa appeared at the door and started walking down the aisle tossing flowers gently in their wake. Next Sonny appeared pulling a wagon with PJ neatly tucked inside holding a silk pillow. Paul couldn't contain himself. The sight of his son caused all of the emotions he was feeling to bubble to the surface and tears escaped from his eyes as he tried to blink them away. Next it was Matt's turn to get emotional as Cami walked down the aisle. He'd never seen her look so beautiful. Her silver silk bridesmaid dress hugged all of her curves and accentuated her tiny waist. Her makeup highlighted her almond shaped eyes and high cheekbones. Matt was so focused on Cami, he didn't even notice when the music changed and Keisha began to walk down the aisle to Beyonce's version of Ave Maria. The entire audience stood up and greeted her as she walked toward her husband. Keisha was so elated. She felt like she was walking in a dream and that the aisle seemed to go on forever. As she got closer to the front she could see that Paul was crying and the sight of tears in his eyes made her eyes well up too but she didn't want to ruin her make-up so she smiled and took a deep breath. Finally, she made it to the front of the room and Paul stepped down to take her hand, he whispered, "you look beautiful babe," and turned to face the minister.

As Paul and Keisha recited their vows Cami couldn't help feeling a little bit jealous. Secretly, she wished that it was her walking

When You Love Somebody

down the aisle to marry Matt. She was so lost in her thoughts that she didn't notice that the ceremony was over and Paul and Keisha were walking down the aisle greeting their guests until Matt came and grabbed her by the hand to walk her down the aisle. He could tell that the ceremony made Cami feel sad so he cracked a joke to try and cheer her up. He loved to see her smile and would give anything to make her happy. He hated that his situation was the cause of her unhappiness. He knew that pretty soon he would have to choose a side but he just hadn't figured out how to deal with Louise yet. She could be vindictive and would make his life hell if he didn't do things the right way. If she ever found out there was another woman involved it would be a wrap but it was becoming harder to hide his feelings for Cami. Everyone in his small circle of friends teased him about how Cami had his nose open.

Now it was Cami's turn to bring Matt back to reality, "Matt let's go. It's picture time."

LatimaNicole

The photographer took what seemed like a thousand pictures positioning the bridal party in various poses. The kids started to get restless so Keisha decided they should head back to the restaurant.

Paul, Keisha and PJ rode in a vintage white Rolls Royce, while Matt, Cami and the kids followed behind in a white stretch Maybach. When they reached the restaurant the drivers let them out the cars and rolled out a white carpet for them to walk on. Paul and Keisha entered the restaurant first as the DJ announced, "Ladies and Gentleman I present to you Mr. and Mrs. Paul Williams."

All of the guests stood and applauded as Paul and Keisha entered the dining area and was ushered to their table.

"Ladies and Gentleman give it up for the bridal party-Matt, Cami, Sonny, Maya, Misa and Paul III."

Cami smiled as she made her way to the bridal table but inside she felt awkward. For some reason she had a strange feeling that someone was watching her but she brushed

When You Love Somebody

it off. "Of course someone is watching you," she told herself, "everyone in the damn room is watching you."

As she sat down the waiter came by with a tray of champagne and she quickly grabbed a glass off of the tray and started to gulp it down but she caught herself, sipped a bit and put the flute down. Keisha nudged her under the table and whispered "what's wrong Cami? You look like you've seen a ghost."

"I don't know Keisha but I feel off, I have a bad feeling in the pit of my stomach and I don't know why."

"Girl it's probably gas." She said laughingly nudging her with her shoulder.

Cami frowned and took another gulp of champagne. She thought to herself that it was a good thing Matt was sitting at the other end of the table next to Paul because she wouldn't be able to hide her mood from him and the last thing they needed was any public displays of affection.

LatimaNicole

She busied herself helping Misa with her food until the Dee Jay announced that it was time for the toasts. Good thing she had something written down because and soon as she heard her name her mind went blank. She took another gulp of champagne, stood up and raised her glass in the air.

"Hello everyone. Thank you so much for coming out and sharing this special moment with Paul and Keisha. For those of you that don't know, technically, I am Keisha's first cousin. Her father and my mother were brother and sister. But we were raised by our grandmother and grew up like sisters." Cami pointed her glass in Keisha's direction and said, "To Keisha, for as long as I can remember you were always the romantic one. You wanted nothing more than to own a restaurant and marry the man of your dreams. I'm proud to say you did both." She then pointed in Paul's direction, "To Paul, Paul, Paul, Paul, I thank you for making my sister-cousin's dreams come true. From the moment you bumped into her in the hallway

When You Love Somebody

at August Martin High School, you two have been inseparable. The both of you have taught me that relationships are not fairy tales, they are real life and there will be ups and downs but when you love somebody you are willing to ride that roller coaster no matter how scary it may seem. I love you guys and I wish you nothing but happiness." When Cami finished her toast the room erupted in applause and she saw a few people dabbing at the corner of their eyes including Paul and Keisha. Next it was Matt's turn to make his toast.

"Ladies and Gentleman, please join me in a toast to the bride and groom, Mr. and Mrs. Paul Williams, everyone raise your glass. I've known Paul since the first grade and not only is he my best friend he is also my brother. Me and this guy have been through so much together and through it all there was always one person who always had his back. Keisha you are the true definition of a partner and I am so happy that my man has you to love him. Now ladies and gentlemen

LatimaNicole

if you don't mind I've prepared a little surprise for the bride and groom for their first dance. Keisha and Paul to the dance floor please"

Paul took Keisha's hand and led her to the dance floor. The band began to play a beautiful ballad. Rasheed and a young lady named Genesis walked onto the stage and stood in front of the microphone stands. Genesis began to hum softly at first and then from somewhere deep in her throat she began to sing the words 'heaven sent'. Rasheed started the first verse and by the time he finished Keisha and Paul were both crying as they held each other in a tight embrace and rocked from side to side. The Dee Jay motioned for the rest of the bridal party to join them so Matt took Cami's hand and led her to the dance floor. Genesis started the second verse as Matt grabbed Cami by the waist and they swayed from side to side. Each couple was so oblivious to the others in the room that they hadn't noticed that Louise had arrived and was

When You Love Somebody

watching Matt and Cami like a hawk. She remembered Cami's face from the picture her girlfriend had sent her a while back. She was a lot of things but she wasn't no fool. If Matt thought he was going to flaunt his whore in her face and in front of her kids he had another thing coming. She didn't give a damn if it was Paul and Keisha's wedding. Fuck them, she thought, with their fake asses, smiling up in her face and they knew all along that Matt was fucking with this bitch. The more she thought about it the madder she got. Finally she got up from her seat and headed for the dance floor.

Matt's dad had been watching Louise ever since she walked in and knew there was going to be trouble so he was already on point when she began making her way over to Matt and Cami. Before she could reach them, Mr. Cortlandt grabbed her by the waist and began dancing with her. She tried to break loose and he tightened his grip.

"Let me go Pop."

LatimaNicole

"What's the matter you don't want to dance with your father-in-law?"

"I need to speak to my husband and the skank bitch he fucking."

"Come on baby girl this ain't the time or the place for all of that. We here to celebrate with Paul and Keisha. All that other drama can wait 'til another time."

"Fuck Paul and Keisha. Them motherfuckers was smiling all up in my face and knew damn well what was going on. That's that phony shit I can't stand."

"Now girl you getting yourself all riled up for nothing. They just dancing. It's tradition."

"Tradition my ass. I see the way he looking at her. He never looked at me like that. When I finish with that bitch she gon think twice about fucking with somebody else's man."

"Calm down Wee. If I don't know nothing about my son, I know that his family means the world to him. Don't do this in front of the kids."

When You Love Somebody

"Fuck that. They need to know how trifling they daddy is. They gon learn today." Louise mustered up all her strength, broke free from her father-in-law and made her way over to Matt and Cami. She came up behind Matt and before Cami could react, Louise punched her in the face. Matt grabbed Louise by her neck but had to catch himself before he choked the life out of her. "Wee what the fuck you doing."

By that time the dance floor was full of guests and it took everyone a minute to realize what was going on. Paul and Keisha rushed over as soon as they realized what was happening. Keisha held Cami back while Paul and Matt restrained Louise. "Bitch you ain't slick but you don fucked the right bitch husband. Let that hoe go Keisha I got something for that ass.

"Really Louise? You doing this at my wedding?"

"You didn't give a fuck about my marriage so why should I care about yours."

"Yo Louise chill the fuck out" Matt said.

LatimaNicole

"Fuck you nigga. I stood by your ass through thick and thin, gave you three babies, put my life on hold and this is the thanks I get. Just let me go so I can drag that bitch across this dance floor."

"Keisha get Cami out of here." Paul said. Keisha tried to get Cami to walk off the dance floor but she wasn't having it.

"Let me go Keish that bitch snuck up and hit me in my face."

"I know sweetie but I'm begging you please don't do this at my wedding. Come on lets go so I can take care of your face."

"Take care of my face? What's wrong with my face Keisha?"

"The bottom of your eye is starting to turn blue and you have a scratch on your cheek that's bleeding a little."

"Oh hell no. I'm gonna kill that bitch."

"No you're not. You're gonna take the L and move on. Now come on let's go."

Cami reluctantly followed Keisha to the restroom. When she got in front of the mirror she screamed out "Oh My God."

When You Love Somebody

Keisha had made it seem like she had a tiny scratch on her cheek and a little bruise under her eye when she really had a cut from the bottom of her eye down to the middle of her cheek and the entire lower part of her eye was black and blue.

"Look at my face Keish." She said as she tried to make her way out of the bathroom. Keisha blocked her from leaving and said "Cami I know you're mad but I need you to take a minute and think about this. If you go out there on some set it off shit you stooping down to her level. You got too much class for that. Now come on and let me clean your face."

Cami reluctantly agreed. Meanwhile back in the dining room, Louise was trying her best to scratch Matt's eyes out. She called him every name in the book and some she must have made up on her own. Mr. Cortlandt and Paul managed to grab hold of her and carried her out of the restaurant. Louise tried to break free but she was no match for the two men who held her under each of her armpits. When they got her outside of the restaurant, they stood her up on her feet. Mr. Cortlandt blocked the entrance to the restaurant so she wouldn't try to get back in.

"Let me go Pop."

"Come on baby girl you gotta get yourself together. You real outta pocket right now and I'm not gonna let you disrespect Paul and Keisha's day not to mention show your ass in front of my grandbabies."

"Paul and Keisha?" "Fuck you Paul and fuck your phony as wife too. Ya'll niggas smiling up in my face and knew damn well my husband was fucking with that hoe."

"First of all," Paul said getting up in Louise's face, "don't you ever call my wife out of her name. Second of all, that man's business is his business. Me and my wife don't have nothing to do with that. You all turnt up for nothing, they was just dancing."

"You must really think I'm fucking stupid Paul. I been down with that nigga for 12 years you think I don't know him by now. I

When You Love Somebody

saw how they were dancing with each other that wasn't just a dance. He fucking her and you can sit there and try to cover for him cause that's what ya'll niggas do but I know the truth. I was with him when he aint have shit on the block doing hand to hand. You forget it was me who let ya'll stash work in my crib. It was me who was on Greyhound taking shit outta state for ya'll. It was me who got pregnant at 17 and got put out her mom's house. That motherfucka owe me and this how he pays me back! Nah I aint having that shit. You think I'm just gonna let a bitch take my husband? Fuck that I got too much time invested in this shit and that bitch needs to know her place. Every time I see that hoe I'm fucking her up on site."

"Louise," Mr. Cortlandt grabbed her by the arm and walked her over to the curb, "listen to me. This aint the time or the place for this. You and Matt need to talk about this at home. You don't need to be putting your business in the street. Now if I was that young lady I would be calling 5-0 to have you arrested for assault. So what you need to do is get in your car and go on home."

The mention of the police seemed to calm Louise down. It never dawned on her that she could be arrested but Pops was right. She needed to get out of there quick just in case them broads tried some corny shit like calling the cops.

"Alright I'm leaving but you tell that piece of shit son of yours he better not bring his ass home tonight cause aint no telling what I might do to him."

She walked across the street and got in her car and sped off. Mr. Cortlandt watched her shaking his head.

"I don't know what my son ever saw in her."

Paul looked at him and said, "well they say hell knows no fury like a woman scorned."

"Aint that the truth."

Matt was about to go look for Cami when he felt a tug on his pants leg.

When You Love Somebody

"Daddy how come mommy hit you and Miss Camille?" Mya asked looking up at her dad with tears in her eyes.

The look on his daughters face gave Matt an instant reality check and he went over to where the kids were and grabbed them all in a big hug.

"I'm sorry you guys had to see that. Your mom is really upset with me right now."

"But if she's mad at you how come she hit Miss Camille?" Sonny asked.

"Probably because the way daddy was dancing with Miss Camille Sonny. Daddy was acting like that was his girlfriend." Mya said twisting her neck.

"Mya what did I tell you about twisting your neck? I don't know why your mom hit Miss Camille but she was wrong, you should only put your hands on someone as a last resort or if they hit you first."

Misa began whining so Matt picked her up.

"Home daddy home."

"Yeah I guess it is about that time. Sonny and Mya go get ya'll stuff so we can go home."

"Home," they said in unison. "Why do we have to go home Dad?" Sonny said.

"Yeah why do we have to go home?" Chimed in Mya, "God mommy and God daddy didn't even cut the cake yet."

Paul and Mr. Cortlandt come back inside the restaurant and headed over to Matt.

"Son are you OK?"

"Yeah dad I'm good. Where is Louise?"

"We convinced her to go home. You got a mess on your hands youngblood. That girl believes what she believes and ain't no talking her out of it."

"Yeah man," Paul chimed in, "Louise was heated. You might get home and all your shit is cut up."

"I ain't worried about Louise. She was dead wrong for coming up in here and disrespecting you and Keisha like that and to top it off she showed her ass in front of my kids."

When You Love Somebody

"Man you know me and Keish gonna ride with you regardless but let me play devil's advocate for a minute. How would you feel if you sat and watched your wife lovingly and affectionately dancing with another man? Women ain't stupid. They can feel when something aint right."

"I feel you man but there is a time and a place for everything. And if that's how she felt then her beef is with me not Cami."

"Man you know I did my share of dirt and one thing I know for sure is when a woman's feelings is involved aint no telling what she would do."

"Youngblood is right son. You need to handle your business but first I think you owe that young lady coming out of the restroom an apology."

Matt looked across the room to see Cami coming out of the bathroom with her hand covering her face. He immediately rushed over to her and opened his mouth to tell her how sorry he was but before he could get a word out Cami interrupted him.

LatimaNicole

"Don't say anything Matt. I don't know how I could have been so stupid to let you into my life I gave you my heart and what did I get in return? A black eye and a cut in my face that I will probably have for the rest of my life."

"I'm so sorry Cami. I never meant for it to come to this. You know I love you and it hurts me to see you hurting. Let me make it better. I promise you won't ever have to worry about her no more. I just need some time to tie up some loose ends."

"You had all the time in the world to get your shit together Matt. I can't do this anymore. I love you but I deserve way more than you can give me. I hope everything works out for you. Good bye."

When You Love Somebody

Chapter 14

Camille

Cami turned and walked toward the door as tears welled up in her eyes. Matt kept calling her but she refused to look back. She kept walking as the wedding guests stared at her shaking their heads. She knew she looked a mess with a black eye and a blood spattered dress but she didn't care, she needed to get home and process the entire ordeal. As she walked out the door and the fresh air hit her face, she could no longer contain herself and the tears flowed. At first tears, then quiet sobs and by the time she was able to flag down a cab she was full blown crying. She sat in the back of the cab as her body heaved from the loud sobs. She couldn't even form the words to tell the cab driver where to take her.

"Are you alright Miss?" The cab driver asked in a heavy Indian accent. "Do you need to go to hospital?"

LatimaNicole

"No, no hospital. Can you please take me to Queens?"

"Okay Miss where in Queens do you want to go?"

"Home. Please take me home."

"You have to tell me where to go to get to your home Miss."

"I'm sorry, the address is 240-24 Oak Park Drive. You can take the Jackie Robinson to the Grand Central."

"Okay Miss just you try to relax. I take you home."

Cami eased back into the plush leather seats and tried to relax. What she really wanted to do was curl up into the fetal position and bawl her eyes out. Her mind replayed her relationship with Matt in scenes as if she were watching a movie.

She remembered when she first met him and she kept telling herself that she didn't date married men. Shen knew then that there was a chemistry between them that she couldn't deny. She always prided herself on being above the bullshit and was never one for

When You Love Somebody

relationship drama. If she had a feeling in her gut that something wasn't right she usually went with it and didn't look back. But Matt was different. He did and said all of the things that she needed for a man to say and do and he seemed so sincere. How could she be so stupid? As a woman how could she come in between another woman's relationship regardless of how good or bad it was especially after seeing what Paul put Keisha through. This was all too much for her to handle right now. She just wanted to go home and get out of her blood stained dress, grab a bottle of wine, lay on her couch and listen to some music.

The cab driver brought her back to reality when he announced, "Miss you are home now."

"Oh okay. How much do I owe you?"

"You owe me nothing. It was pleasure to make sure you home safe. I have daughter and it is a man's job to protect the woman. You be strong and get rest tomorrow will be better day yes."

LatimaNicole

Cami was so touched by the cab driver's words that a fresh stream of tears started to flow. "Thank you so much sir."

When she got out of the car she realized that in her hurry to get out of the restaurant, she never got any of her belongings. Good thing the driver wouldn't take any money from her because she left her pocketbook at the hotel with all her cash, credit cards and keys. When she realized she had no keys to get into her house she sat on the stoop and put her head in her hands.

"This is fucking great," she mumbled under her breath, "how in the hell am I supposed to get in?"

It was late on a Saturday afternoon so she knew the maintenance office was closed and the emergency number was tacked up on her bulletin board in the kitchen. This was one time she wished she had taken the time to get to know her neighbors at least then she would have had somewhere to go to use a phone or something. As she sat there trying to figure out what she was going to do, she

When You Love Somebody

remembered that her basement window was open. She looked up and down the block to make sure no one was watching or driving by and then got on all fours and tried to climb through the window but it wasn't open wide enough. The damn latch was on that stopped the window from sliding completely open.

"Damn it," she yelled in frustration.

She got up and started looking around for a rock to break the window when a car pulled into her driveway.

"Hey young lady I figured you might need this." Mr. Cortlandt held up Cami's pocketbook as he rolled down the passenger window.

"Mr. Cortlandt what are you doing here? How did you know where I lived?"

"Matt was going to bring your stuff over to you but I told him it would probably be better if he didn't so he gave me the address and here I am."

"Thank you so much. I really appreciate you doing this for me. I'm sorry for

LatimaNicole

everything that happened especially with the babies being there. I know they must have a ton of questions."

"Don't you worry about them, their parents are going to have to sit them down and have a talk with them and they'll be alright. The question is how are you doing? That cut on your face looks like it might need a stitch or two."

"I don't think so. I think when she hit me her ring scratched my face that's all. But thank you for your concern."

"Listen Cami, I know how my son feels about you. Hell anybody that's been around the two of you could tell how ya'll feel about each other. I been told that boy he needed to either shit or get off the pot. It aint fair to nobody to drag the situation out now he got two women hurting because he thought he had time to do things his way. I aint never been one to speak on another man's situation and I aint gonna start now so let me just make sure you get in the house okay and then I'm gone."

When You Love Somebody

"I appreciate you Mr. Cortlandt. I'm just as guilty as Matt in this whole thing. I knew he was married from the beginning, he never lied to me about anything. I think that's the worst part of it all. I knew and I still allowed myself to get caught up."

"Well baby girl the only thing I can tell you is that you don't get to choose who you fall in love with and sometimes the situation is not the greatest and you have to fight for it and other times it may seem like the perfect situation and then it all falls apart. That's life."

Cami reached in her bag, took out her key and opened the door.

"Would you like to come in? Can I get you something to drink?"

"Naw I think I better head back. I got a feeling I'm gonna need to hang out with my grand babies tonight."

"Okay well please tell them I'm sorry and that I'm alright."

"Will do. Take care of yourself young lady."

LatimaNicole

Cami smiled at Matt's father as he turned and walked away. She closed the door, deactivated the alarm and slid down the door onto the floor and the tears started flowing all over again. After being on the floor for what seemed like an eternity she got up, took her dress off and threw it in the garbage. As she was making her way up the stairs to the bedroom her house phone rang. She looked at the caller ID and saw that it was Keisha.

"Hello."

"Oh my goodness Cami are you okay?"

"Yes I'm fine. I just got in the house. I didn't have anything with me. Thank God for the cab driver and Matt's dad or I would be stranded somewhere."

"Do you need me to come over?"

"Girl don't be silly. It's bad enough I ruined your wedding, I'm not going to mess up your honeymoon too."

"It's no big deal Paul and I didn't have any real plans. We were just going to stay the

When You Love Somebody

night at the hotel. But PJ and I can come spend the night with you."

"You know you guys are always welcome but I wouldn't be good company and I just want to take a shower and get some rest."

"Are you sure?"

"Yes. I'll be fine. I'll give you a call in the morning."

"Okay. I love you sister-cousin."

"I love you too. Talk to you later."

Cami hung up the phone and went upstairs to her bedroom. There were reminders of Matt everywhere she looked. On her dresser was a picture of her and him being silly in the photo booth at the movies. On her chaise was the blanket they used when they had a picnic in the park. She felt the urge to pull an Angela Bassett in Waiting to Exhale and take anything that reminded her of Matt in the backyard and burn it. Unfortunately she couldn't burn him out of her heart and mind. She walked into her master bath chiding herself for having been so stupid but that was water under the bridge. She vowed to

LatimaNicole

never allow herself to get caught up like that again. While she waited for the tub to fill up she looked in the mirror. Her face was an absolute mess. She had to laugh to herself, "that bitch got me good," she said to the mirror. But she couldn't blame Louise. She probably would have done the same thing if she saw her husband all boo'd up with another woman. Cami turned away from the mirror and added some lavender oil to her bath water and stepped in the tub. The heat from the water and the calming scent of the lavender forced her to relax and pretty soon she was fast asleep.

When You Love Somebody

Chapter 14

Matthew

"Yo P it's Matt."

"What up man? How you?"

"I'm good but have you and Keisha heard from Cami? I been trying to call her but she keeps sending me to voicemail."

"Keisha spoke to her she said she was good she just needed some rest."

"She can't be good man. I know I fucked up and she got caught up in my bullshit."

"Give her some space, she probably needs to get her mind right."

"Yeah I know but I can't stand knowing that she's hurting because of me. "What can I do to make it right?"

"It's really nothing you can do. Cami is not the type of chick you can throw a bag or a pair of shoes at and everything will be okay. The more you sweat her the more she's gonna pull away. "

"Damn P I can't just sit here and do nothing. I can't just let her walk away like that."

LatimaNicole

"Man chill out. What you need to be doing is getting your house in order."

"On the real I don't even want to deal with Louise. I can't stand to look at her. I know she's the mother of my kids but I didn't marry her for love. Over time I grew to love her but I was never in love with her. I just did what I thought was best for my kids and after a while I just got comfortable and settled. You know she was never the mothering type. She's always been more focused on shopping and hanging out with her girlfriends than she is on making sure the kids' homework was done or making them something to eat. It's like after I started making some real paper, she felt like she didn't have to do anything but spend my money. She's never worked a day in her life. I've always taken care of her. She's spoiled and selfish and I just can't do it no more man. Did I tell you that I walked in on her talking to one of her friends on the phone and this broad was saying Matt ain't going nowhere and she actually had the dirty nerve

When You Love Somebody

to tell her if I even thought about cheating on her she would put a hole in the condom like she did the last time. I haven't slept with her since. What type of shit is that man? Basically she taking me for granted because she know how much I love my babies."

"Damn man that's that bullshit."

"Word. I just gotta figure out how I'm gonna make my move without hurting the kids. You know how I feel about them growing up with both their parents in the same house."

"Man listen I grew up with both my parents in the same house and look at how I turned out. My Pops probably would have did us a favor if he would have bounced. The sad part is my Moms knew all the dirt he was doing in the street and she always let him come back home so I grew up thinking that a real man was supposed to have a bunch of different women and one main chick to hold him down. I remember my Pops taking me with him to see his other women. I would either sit in the car with some McDonalds or

in the living room of the lady's crib while
they were in the bedroom getting busy. My
Pops was ruthless. He had women calling
and coming by the crib and my Moms would
beef and cry and put him out for a while but
he would always come back. He would chill
for a minute and then it was back to his
same old ways. It wasn't until Keisha had PJ
that I realized that I was doing the same shit.
I didn't want my seed growing up around
that type of environment. Plus Keisha is a
good girl. On some real shit she should have
left me a long time ago with all the bullshit I
put her through."

"That's what I'm talking about. Keisha
stuck by your side and supported you even
when you aint have shit.

"Do you love Cami man?"

"Damn yo. Right person at the wrong time.
Ain't life a bitch?"

"Tell me about it. If I could just talk to her I
know we could work it out."

"Yo you my man and I love you like a
brother so you know I ain't gonna sugar coat

When You Love Somebody

shit for you. On some real shit. Work what out? You being selfish. Think about if it was Maya or Misa messing with a married dude, what would you be telling them?

"Oh so you finally get your shit together and now you want to give advice? Get the fuck outta here man. I ain't tryna hear that shit. I just need my girl back. All that other shit you talking, you can tell your story walking."

"My man I ain't the enemy. Your girl? Are you fucking serious? Did you forget about your wife nigga? You ain't built for this shit homie so cut your losses and move on. How long did you think she was gonna play house with you? Cami ain't that type of broad and obviously you ain't that nigga so you need to dead that shit you talking."

"Fuck you P."

"Yo we've been friends since first grade. We been through the trenches together. If I can't call you on your shit then who can? You lucky I got love for you because if it was any other nigga that would've

LatimaNicole

disrespected me like you just did they would
be kissing the carpet right about now. On
that note I'm out."

"Yeah aight."

When You Love Somebody

Chapter 15

Camille

"Why don't you just talk to him Cami?"

"And say what Keish?"

"Don't say anything, just listen to what he has to say."

"I already know what he's gonna say. I'm sorry baby. You know I love you. I just need some time to figure this out. I gotta make sure my kids is straight blah blah blah."

"So that's it. You're throwing in the towel?"

"Towel? Hell I'm waving the white flag. I give up. I'm tired Keisha. I can't do it, never could. I always knew the day would come but I convinced myself to ride it til the wheels fell off and girl I'm sitting on bricks right now."

"If you love him then you have to fight for him Cami. Nothing worth having is gonna come easy."

LatimaNicole

"What are you saying Keisha? That I deserve to spend the rest of my life as somebody's mistress?"

"That's not what I meant and you know it. I know for a fact that you love him and he loves you. The chemistry you two have with each other is crazy. I've never seen him like that with anyone else."

"Is that supposed to make it all better?"

"Hell I don't know. I can't even believe I'm saying this to you after all the mess Paul put me through. Speaking of Paul, he told me that him and Matt got into it the other day. He was so upset he said if Matt wasn't his boy he would have laid him out."

"What happened?"

"Apparently Matt was telling him how much he loved you and wanted you back and Paul was telling him that he needs to either shit or get off the pot and he told Paul 'fuck you'."

"He must have hit a nerve."

"Must have because Matt don't even talk like that."

When You Love Somebody

"Well it don't matter anyway. I bowed out gracefully. Let that woman have her husband in peace."

"But what if her husband doesn't want her?"

"Well then he should have made a move I can't live my life in limbo I'm getting older and I want to settle down with someone that can commit to me one hundred percent. What I look like being the side chick at fifty years old?"

"I hear you girl but you know I'm a romantic at heart and I know love when I see it. What you and Matt have is special. It reminds me of Grandma and Grandpa."

"Oh please now you're trying to beat me over the head."

"I'm serious. Just think about it Cami. I gotta go. I just came by to check on you. I gotta get back to PJ I don't like leaving him with the nanny for too long. Love you. You should come by the restaurant and hang out with me one day this week."

"I love you too but I don't think I'm ready to return to the scene of the crime just yet."

LatimaNicole

"Well if you want to get on with your life like you say you do you can't stay cooped up in this house every day."

"I'm not cooped up. I go out."

"Where? To work? That don't count."

"I'll think about it. I'll call you and let you know."

"I know what that means."

"You don't know nothing. I'll talk to you later now get out."

Cami shut the door, closed her eyes and took a deep breath. She then looked up to the ceiling and whispered, "Please Lord give me strength to do the right thing". She walked into the kitchen and poured herself a glass of wine, leaned against the coolness of her quartz countertop, picked up the remote to the stereo system and pressed shuffle then play on her Ipod. The first song to come on was Aretha Franklin's 'It Hurts Like Hell' from the Waiting to Exhale soundtrack. As the lyrics blared through the speakers Cami could feel the words speaking to her soul.

When You Love Somebody

Sometimes it hurts to love so bad

(when you know you've given it your best)

Sometimes it hurts to even laugh

(you feel a thousand miles from happiness)

Sometimes the pain is just too much

And it hurts like hell

That's the way it feels

As the song ended she walked into the living room and sat down on the calf skin rug. The same rug that she and Matt had made love on more times than she cared to think about right now. The next song to come on was 'Faded Pictures' by Case and Joe.

She was more than a woman, a goddess for all it seems

And all I ever needed was her right here loving me

For a while we were cool and the grooving of love was on

But I still remember how it felt when our love was gone

In a tattered picture book

Was a photograph she took years ago

Secret memories in her mind

LatimaNicole

How could love be so unkind?
Heartbreak time
She never realized how sad these songs were
before now. She had always loved good
RnB music but she must have never really
paid attention to the lyrics because her
favorite artists were speaking to her pain
right now. The next song to come on 'When
You Love Somebody' by Leelah James sent
her over the edge. She couldn't hold back
the tears as Leelah's deep soulful voice
sang,

What is a woman
To do with a man
Who treats her unkindly
When she's down, all she can
I cried so many nights
How we fuss and fight
The make ups and the break ups
I loved you and only you
The things you do
When you love somebody
When you love somebody
I gave you my lovin'

When You Love Somebody

With no questions asked

Tears on my pillow

From all your disrespect

I didn't care about your past

I only wanted to make us last

And oooohhh

I loved you and only you

The things you do

When you love somebody

Oh love, yeah, um

When you love somebody

I loved you baby

Nooo

When you love somebody

When you love somebody

The things you do

For love

Ooh

The things that you do yeah

Who knows what tomorrow may bring me

All I know is it is what it is

And why, do I look for clues, y'all?

When I don't have to question you

When you love somebody

LatimaNicole

When you love somebody

Y'all hear me

The things you do

All in the name of love

All in the name of love

In the name of love

All the things you do for love

Love love love

It's in the name of love

The things you do for love

Love, love, love

Love somebody, love somebody, love

somebody

When the song ended she looked at the glass
in her hand and hurled it across the room.
She fantasized that the wall was Matt's head
and the crimson liquid that splattered and
dripped down her platinum colored walls
was Matt's blood. She didn't ever remember
being so angry and hurt at the same time.
But could she really blame Matt? He had
never made her any promises and he was
always truthful with her. She knew his
situation from the beginning. The more she

When You Love Somebody

thought about it, the more she realized she wasn't really mad at Matt, she was angry with herself for letting things get as far as they had. She knew she was a good woman and any sane man should have been happy to have her in his life. Problem was she always fell for the men with baggage. Whether it was emotional, financial or familial, it all amounted to dead weight and she was tired of having to share in carrying the load. So she did what she always did when she had enough. She tucked her feelings away in the deep recesses of her heart and pretended that everything was all good.

Chapter 16

Matthew

"Cami its Matt please call me back and let me know you're okay. Baby you know I love you. Please just talk to me. We can get past this I know we can. Please just call me back."

Matt hung up the phone and put his head in his hands. He didn't even hear Louise come into the kitchen.

"Oh so you loving bitches now huh?"

He looked up just in time to block Louise' fist as she tried to connect with the side of his head.

"Yo Wee keep your hands to yourself. If you want to talk like two adults we can do that but you not gonna be putting your hands on me."

"Fuck you Matt. We ain't got shit to talk about. After all I did for you this how you pay me back? If it wasn't for me you wouldn't be shit and now that you got a lil

When You Love Somebody

paper you think your shit don't stink. Niggas kill me. Where was that bitch when you needed your work bagged up? Where was she when you needed someone to take Greyhound outta town with a duffle bag full of crack? Nigga I put my freedom on the line for you."

"That was your choice. I never made you do anything and don't act like you ain't benefit from any paper I ever made. Who was driving to high school in a BMW wearing all the flyest designer shit? Who was up in the club every weekend spending bread like it was going out of style? For somebody who never had a job a damn day in their life you seem to have done pretty good for yourself."

"You damn right I never had a job. I had your kids, that's the only fucking job I needed."

"You so trifling. Don't think I don't know about you putting holes in the condoms. Fuck was that about? You're selfish ass don't even do shit with the kids so what work are you doing? I can count on one

hand how many times you went up to their
school. Shit you probably don't even know
their teachers' names."

"So fucking what. That's what you're here
for Mr. World's Greatest Dad."

"Do you even love your kids or did you
have them to keep me around."

"Nigga don't flatter yourself. How dare you
ask me if I love my kids? You got some
fucking nerve. I should be asking you that
question since you willing to risk losing
your family for a side bitch."

"You got one more time to call her a bitch."

"Or what? You gonna stand in my face and
defend that hoe? Oh I know you done lost
your fucking mind. Pack your shit and get
the fuck out of my house."

"Your house? Please you mean my house. If
anybody is leaving it's gonna be you. I
wouldn't leave my kids with you if you was
the last person on earth. Maybe you need to
go stay with one of your stank ass home
girls for a couple of days until you cool off
and think about what you saying and who

When You Love Somebody

you saying it to. You don't have shit, ain't ever gonna have shit and won't ever be shit because you too busy tryna come up off somebody else that it never dawned on you to get your own shit just in case."

"I fucking hate you. You bastard. I'm your wife and that's how you talk to me? Oh trust me motherfucker this ain't over. You gonna get yours."

Matt picked Louise up and sat her on top of the huge kitchen island. He put his face so close to hers that their foreheads were almost touching. Through clenched teeth he said, "don't you ever fucking threaten me I will make your life a living hell. Try me if you want to. Now I'm going to pick MY kids up from school and when we get back your ass better not be here".

Matt walked out of the kitchen leaving Louise sitting on the island too stunned to move.

She didn't know how long she had been sitting there but her legs had begun to get numb and she could feel that annoying tingling sensation traveling from her knees to the tips of her toes. She tried to hop down but her legs wouldn't cooperate so she tried inching toward the edge of the island and sliding down. That wasn't working either. She had always prided herself in her 5'4" 115 pound petite frame but at this moment she wished she were about 5" taller so that at least her feet would touch the floor when she shimmied to the edge.

"Wee what you doing up there baby girl," Mr. Cortlandt asked as he walked toward her.

"Can you help me down Pop? Your damn son done lost his fucking mind."

Mr. Cortlandt lifted her off of the island and ease her gently to the floor but as soon as her feet hit the tile her knees buckled and she began to go down.

"Whoa baby girl I got you. Here why don't you sit in this chair and tell me what's going on."

"I walked in on your son leaving that bitch a message talking about he love her and I lost

When You Love Somebody

it. Then he had the nerve to take up for her so I told him to get the fuck out. You know what this motherfucker said to me? 'This is his house and that I had to be out by the time he got back from picking the kids up' Ain't that some shit? I'm his fucking wife and he kicking me to the curb for some random stank ass bitch. I'm not having it. I got some shit for his ass when he get back. He must have forgot who he fucking with."

Mr. Cortlandt looked at her and shook his head. It's always the short ones with the most mouth he thought to himself. He took a deep breath and rubbed his temples.

"Listen here baby girl, I try my best not to get in ya'lls business so I'm just gonna say this one thing and them I'm gonna leave it alone. You and Matt got married for the wrong reasons. He married you because you were pregnant and you married him because you wanted the lifestyle he could provide for you. Now somewhere down the line you probably grew to love one another but were you ever in love with each other? Are you

showing that unconditional love to your
children? For the little bit of time I've been
here I've noticed that there is no affection
between the two of you, it seems to me like
it's more of a business arrangement than
anything else. Now if you want something
different you've got to do something
different. Now I'm not blaming you or
anything like that. It takes two to tango. But
what I am saying is if you want your
husband and your family you have to fight
for it. Not with your fists baby Frazier, but
with your actions. You have to make the
commitment and do the work it's gonna take
to make it right."

He reached over the table and squeezed
Louise's hand and tears welled up in her
eyes.

"Did you know Matt is the only man I have
ever been with? Sure I have flirted and even
went out on a couple of dates with guys but
I've never slept with anybody but him. I was
young when I met him and only seventeen
when I got pregnant. I had no business

When You Love Somebody

being married with a baby at that age. My mother kicked me out when she found out I was pregnant and it's been me, Matt and the kids ever since. I refuse to let the next chick take my life from me. Oh trust me I am gonna win this one."

"There's no winners or losers here. That's your problem baby girl, you keep thinking about yourself. Put yourself in your husband's shoes. Think about what he needs as a man and give it to him. Put your ego to the side and humble yourself if you want to save your marriage. Now I suggest that you give him some time to get his mind right. Maybe you should take a little vacation or something. The time apart will do you both some good."

They both looked up as the kids came running in the kitchen.

"Mommy" they yelled in unison.

Misa the ever sensitive one sensed that something wasn't right and immediately went over to her mother.

LatimaNicole

"Mommy why come you crying." She said as she put her index finger on Louise's cheek.

"I'm ok baby me and your Pop Pop was just talking and I got a little sad."

"I don't want you to be sad mommy. You supposed to be happy because when you're sad it makes me sad."

"Ok lil mama I'm not sad anymore and you don't be sad either."

Mr. Cortlandt got up and said, "come on you guys let's go upstairs and put your stuff away. Who wants to go get ice cream?"

The kids ran upstairs leaving a trail of meeeeeeeees floating in the air. Mr. Cortlandt walked passed Matt and whispered, "Listen to what she has to say," as he went upstairs to join his grandchildren.

"I thought I told you to be gone before I got back," Matt said through clenched teeth.

Louise was ready to go for Matt's jugular but she stopped herself remembering what her father-in-law said.

When You Love Somebody

"Matt I don't want to fight with you. I think we both need some time apart so what can think. I'm gonna go stay with Sharice for a couple of days, maybe fly down to Miami for the weekend and do some soul searching. But don't get it twisted, I'm not leaving my home or my kids."

"Do whatever you gotta do it's not like you been there for us anyway. The kids won't miss you."

"What did I ever do to you that was so bad that you coming out of pocket like this?"

"Nothing. That's the problem, you've done nothing unless you benefitted from it. You know what, I'm done with this conversation I'm going to the studio. Tell Pop to hold the kids down for me. Have fun soul searching in Miami."

He curled his fingers up into mock quotation marks as he walked out the door."

Louise was stunned. She had never seen this side of Matt. His mild mannerisms and laid back attitude was a stark contrast to her loud get in someone's face in a heartbeat persona.

LatimaNicole

She shook her head in part shame, part disbelief as she realized she had made the huge mistake of underestimating Matt.

When You Love Somebody

Chapter 16

Camille

Cami locked the door to her studio and decided she would go to the restaurant and surprise Keisha with a visit and get her some crab cakes and macaroni and cheese. As soon as she got in the car her phone rang. She looked at the caller ID and didn't recognize the number so she let the call go to voicemail. She slipped Mary J Blige's latest CD in the CD changer and made her way to Brooklyn. Her phone rang again, she looked at the screen and it was the same number as the last call. She let it go to voicemail thinking it was probably Matt calling from a different number hoping she would answer. She wasn't falling for that trick so she turned up the volume and sang along with Mary and Drake.

Don't it seem like, like I'm always there
when it matters
But missing most of the other time, a terrible
pattern

LatimaNicole

*The rewards I see from working made me
an addict*
*Theres way more people that want it than
people that have it*
*I dont get it, I would hate to think I tricked
'em*
*They fall victim to my system, guess I sure
know how to pick 'em*
*And I'm always her regret, yeah, I'm always
her regret*
*And I always make it harder on whoever's
coming next*
It goes up and down, it's just up and down
She's crying now but she'll laugh again
Cause we on the rise and she here with us
In expensive shit, just keeps happening
*She loves it, she stares at me like who does
this*
*And we hold hands while I pray that she's
not the type to hold grudges*
I'm wrong..
Bad boys aint no good
Good boys aint no fun
Lord knows that I should

When You Love Somebody

Run off with the right one

Me and Mr. Wrong get along so good

Even though he breaks my heart so bad

We got a special thing going on

Me and Mr. Mister Wrong

Even if I try, no, I never could

Give him up cause his loves like that

Aint no way that I'm moving on

I love my Mr. Wrong

Hung up off your good

You call and I run

My family's screaming at me don't do it

Don't do it Mary

I guess they never had none

When he put that loving on me, I can't think

of nothing

That'll make me walk out

I'm holding on

I love my Mr. Wrong

He be kissing and touching on me

I can't help but love him

I must be out my mind

For going so strong

I love my Mr. Wrong

LatimaNicole

Me and Mr. Wrong get along so good
Even though he breaks my heart so bad
We got a special thing going on
Me and Mr. Wrong,
Even if I try, no, I never could
Give him up cause his loves like that
Ain't no way that I'm moving on
I love my Mr. Wrong

There was something about a Mary J. Blige song that could speak to any love situation at any point in your life, Cami thought to herself. As the music continued to play Cami realized that she was crying. She chided herself for still being emotional over Matt. How could she be so in love with a man who would never be able to give her the love she knew she deserved? She turned onto Dekalb Avenue and to her surprise she saw a car pulling out of a spot a few doors down from the front entrance of Keisha's restaurant. This must be my lucky day, she mused. She slowed down and put her signal on to let the cars behind her know she was waiting for the spot. Something about the

When You Love Somebody

car looked familiar to her. When the car pulled out she realized that it was Matt's car. Thank goodness he hadn't seen her. She was not ready emotionally to be in his presence. If she was honest with herself she would have to admit that he still made her weak. After she parked, she sat in the car for a few minutes to gather her composure and put her game face on. She mentally prepared herself for the questions Keisha was sure to throw her way. Keisha had a way of piercing her to the core and she always knew when she was lying. She had a trick for her today though, she had worn her midnight black tinted Tom Ford sunglasses and she planned on wearing them the entire time she was in the restaurant.

She was expecting to see the hostess when she walked in but instead she ran dead smack into Keisha.

"Well well well. Look what the cat drug in?"

"Oh shut up and get me a table."

LatimaNicole

"I know this long lost heifer ain't up in my restaurant trying to tell me what to do."

"Alright Keisha. Give it a rest. You know how I get when I'm going through something. So why are you acting like that?"

"What you're going through don't have nothing to do with me or your God-son. He probably wouldn't even know who you were if he saw you."

"I know, I know. I promise to do better. That's why I'm here. I miss you sister-cousin."

"Whatever. Come on let's grab a seat. By the way you have perfect timing."

"Why you say that?"

"Because Matt just left."

"Yeah I actually saw him pulling out and took his parking spot."

"Oh goodness. Did he see you?"

"I don't think so. I waited a couple of spots back."

"You really need to talk to him Cami."

"I can't Keish. I don't have the will power right now. If I saw him I would want to hug

When You Love Somebody

him and touch him and that would lead to us having sex. I can't risk it."

"I didn't say you had to talk to him in person. Give him a call. You need to have some closure."

"The problem with closure is that it's so final. My brain is telling me it's over but my heart is telling me to fight for us. It's just too much for me right now."

"Well the only way you're going to know if there is anything worth fighting for is if you talk to him. You never know he could have filed for divorce and is just waiting on you so ya'll can live happily ever after."

Cami was shocked by Keisha's words. Did she know something that she didn't? Did Matt confide in her? Her mind was going in so many different directions that she had drowned out the rest of what Keisha was saying. She saw her mouth moving but she couldn't process any of her words.

"Cami are you listening to me?"

"Sorry what did you say?"

LatimaNicole

"I said Matt didn't say much when he came in today other than asking me did I speak to you. I told him that I had and we were getting ready to leave for the Essence Festival."

"You told him I would be in New Orleans? Why would you do that?"

"What? I said something wrong?"

"Now you know damn well he's gonna find a reason to be in New Orleans next week."

Keisha tried to hide the smirk on her face but Cami caught it, reached over the table and swatted her with a napkin.

"You dirty heifer! You told him on purpose."

"I have no idea what you're talking about Camille."

Keisha couldn't hold her laughter in anymore and let out a barrage of girlish giggles. She had decided that she needed to intervene and play cupid because Cami could be too stubborn for her own good. When her mind was set on something it damn near took an act of congress to get her

When You Love Somebody

to change it. She usually gave guys one chance and if they messed up that was it. There was no going back for her. She didn't believe in mistakes when it came to relationships and Keisha was trying to get her to see that no relationship was perfect. It took a lot of hard work, compromise and sacrifice to make one work and she had never seen Cami put in the effort to sustain a relationship once her mate did something wrong.

"Alright play dumb. Don't worry I got something for you. Just wait until we get on that plane."

"By the way what time is our flight again?

"American Airlines flight 2970 leaving from JFK at 8AM. You better not be late either. You know how security is at the airport. I would hate to have to leave your slow behind."

"Don't worry, I'll be on time. I wouldn't miss this trip for the world. I got a feeling something big is going to happen."

LatimaNicole

"Yeah ok. See you and your feelings on Thursday."

Cami got up and walked out of the restaurant. She walked down Dekalb and made a left on Clermont. She always walked this neighborhood when she wanted to clear her head. The blocks were filled with turn of the century brownstones that for the most part were still in their original condition. Before her parents died, they had lived in a brownstone in Bed-Stuy and she remembered sitting on her stoop with her mom eating ice-cream or getting her hair braided. She often wondered what her parents would think of how her life was turning out. She hoped they would be proud of her. She knew for sure her dad wouldn't have liked Matt. No one would have been good enough for his baby girl, but Matt being married was definitely something he wouldn't have approved of. Come to think of it, Matt reminded her of her father. He had the same laid back demeanor and adoration for his daughters that her father

When You Love Somebody

had. She thought to herself that it must have been true what they said about women falling for men that were like their fathers. She continued on Clermont until she hit Fulton, made a left and walked down Vanderbilt until she was back on Dekalb. That was her exercise for the day. She was going to go home pack and take a shower. She was happy she had cleared her schedule for the week and wasn't teaching summer classes. She needed a break. Struggling with her feelings for Matt was really taking a toll on her. She was hardly getting any sleep. Most nights she either walked the floors of her house or found something that needed immediate cleaning in the middle of night. She didn't know how this thing with Matt was going to play out but she knew one thing….Something had to give.

Chapter 17

Matthew

Matt walked out of the Louis Armstrong International Airport in New Orleans and was immediately assaulted by the humidity that hung over the airport like a wet blanket. Thank goodness his driver was pulling up in a black and chrome Cadillac Escalade ESV. The driver got out of the truck and grabbed his bags. Matt was about to get into the back of the truck when his phone rang.

"Hello."

"What's up Matt?"

"What's the deal Ra? Did you touch down yet?"

"Yeah man I touched down about an hour ago. Guess who was on my flight?"

"Who?"

"Your man Paul, his wife and her cousin."

"Oh word?"

"Yo the cousin is official. I'm definitely gonna holla at her while we down here. I

When You Love Somebody

know she got that good good. Chicks with hazel eyes always got good cooch."

Matt gritted his teeth and tried to calm himself down. Rasheed didn't know about him and Cami, he was just talking the way most men do but Matt was thankful he was on the phone and not standing there in person because he probably would have punched him in his mouth.

"Yo Ra man chill with all that."

"That's you man?"

"Something like that."

"My bad man. No disrespect. I didn't know."

"Don't sweat it. As long as you don't cross that line we good."

"Nah man you know I don't rock like that. We peoples I would never go against the grain."

"Aight man I'm on my way to the hotel. What time is your rehearsal?"

"It's at 4. I'm gonna go grab a bite to eat and then head over to the Superdome."

LatimaNicole

"Aight yo. I'm gonna check in, take a shower and then I'll meet you there."

"No doubt. Yo man again my bad. Why didn't you tell me you was hitting that?"

"I thought you knew from the wedding."

"Nah man, what happened at the wedding?"

"I don't want to get into that but we've been rocking for a minute now."

"I like your style my dude. You be on the low with your shit. I been working with you for almost a year now and you never mentioned her or any other chick to me."

"I like to keep my personal life personal."

"I hear that hot shit. Aight then later my dude."

"One."

Matt sat in the back of the truck thinking about how many other men had tried to get at Cami. He wasn't the jealous type but for some reason the thought of Cami being with another man was enough to send him over the edge. He still hadn't quite worked things out with Louise. After he kicked her out she did a complete 180 and started spending

When You Love Somebody

more time with the kids, cooking dinner and even checking for him throughout the day. She even made attempts to communicate with him. To top it off she hadn't hung out with her girlfriends in the last month. Matt's question was how long was she going to keep it up? Louise was the type of person that would do whatever she had to in order to get what she wanted. He figured that as soon as he let his guard down she would go right back to her old ways and he wasn't trying to go there with her.

By the time the SUV pulled up in front of the hotel it had to be about 100 degrees. Matt tipped the driver as the bell hop got his bags out of the truck. He made a beeline straight for the hotel lobby. The hotel was nice and cool and the young lady at the front desk seemed to be a bit smitten with Matt so she upgraded his room to a deluxe suite for no extra charge and wrote her phone number on the room key envelope. Matt laughed at the fact that he still had it. However, he had no intentions of calling the young lady back. He had enough drama in his life.

As soon as he got in the room the phone rang. He wondered who could be calling the room since he had just checked in and hadn't given anyone the room number yet.

"Hello."

"Hello Mr. Cortlandt. This is Starkeisha from the front desk. I was calling to let you know that if you needed anything, and I do mean anything, please don't hesitate to give the front desk a call. I will be here until 10 and it would be my pleasure to make sure your stay at the Hyatt Regency is a memorable one."

Matt looked at the receiver in disbelief. He had always heard that southern woman were aggressive but damn.

"I appreciate your hospitality and I will be sure to ring the front desk if I have any issues. Thank you."

"No thank you for choosing the Hyatt Regency. I look forward to seeing you soon."

When You Love Somebody

Talk about forward. Matt thought to himself. He would make it his business to stay away from the front desk while she was working. Women who were aggressive and extra were a turn off for him. He liked to do the pursuing. The way he saw it, if a woman was bold enough to flirt with him and risk losing her job, she wasn't his kind of woman. He already had a leech at home and he sure as hell didn't need another one. Cami was the exact opposite she had a quiet sensuality that you couldn't ignore. She never tried too hard to be seen, in fact most times she would rather play the background. But once she caught your attention there was no denying how sexy she was.

Matt shook his head and decided to go take a shower to cool off. He turned the water on and let it run while he got his Gucci toiletries bag out of his luggage. When he stepped in the shower, he recalled one of the times he and Cami had taken a shower together. The memory aroused him so much that his penis began to grow while the water beat against his throbbing veins. It had been a while since he had had any sex and he was horny as hell. He started stroking his dick while imagining it was Cami's mouth that was providing the pleasure instead of his five fingers. As his pleasure increased, so did his speed. He continued to stroke himself up and down in a rapid motion until he felt himself about to go over the edge. He thought about how wet Cami's pussy would feel whenever he would enter her and the vision drove him right to a powerful orgasm. His thick semen poured out of him with such force that it made his legs weak and he had to sit down on the edge of the tub to finish releasing. His orgasm was so intense that all he could do was sit there and watch the water wash his seed down the drain. He thought to himself that he had had enough of not being with Cami. He was going to find her while he was here in the Big Easy and beg her to come back to him. He needed her. Everything was off kilter since Cami ended their affair and he needed her back in his

When You Love Somebody

life. She brought a calm and balance to his spirit that he had never known before. He missed that. And he missed her. He finished his shower, stepped out the tub and wrapped a towel around his waist. After wiping the steam off of the mirror he took a good look at his face. He wasn't a bad looking dude but he noticed that he had begun to look older than his 37 years. He hadn't been getting enough sleep lately. It was hard. When his head hit the pillow all he could think about was Cami and he wound up tossing and turning all night so to keep his mind off of her he stayed in the studio and worked until it was time to get the kids ready for school. He could feel the exhaustion catching up with him though so he laid across the bed and passed out.

Chapter 18

Camille

Camille, Keisha and Paul had finally made it to New Orleans. That was the worst flight she had ever been on. The airline overbooked, there were not one but three screaming babies on the flight and even though she was flying first class, she still wasn't comfortable. The man sitting next to her had taken off his shoes and unbuckled his belt like he was at home or something and then went to sleep and started snoring so loud the flight attendant had to nudge him a few times to wake him up. She was so through by the time her flight landed that all she wanted to do was get to her hotel and take a nap. She had been sleeping a lot lately and she knew that excessive sleeping was a sign of depression. She had been down in the dumps ever since Keisha's wedding but something else was off. She just couldn't put her finger on it. She was normally a very patient person, especially with her clients

When You Love Somebody

but lately she found herself even being aggravated at work. Keisha told her to go see the doctor and get a complete work up but deep down she already knew what was going on with her she just didn't want to admit it. Cami was pregnant. She hadn't taken a test or anything but she knew her body and if she couldn't count on anything else she could count on menstruating every 28 days. It had been six weeks since her last period and if her calculations were correct, that was the last time she and Matt had made love. He insisted on removing the condom and she like a fool let him. As soon as he entered her raw they both began to orgasm and she didn't let him pull out. She was so disappointed in herself for being so reckless. But what was done was done and she couldn't go back and change it. She would deal with everything when she got back to New York. For now she just wanted to focus on work and having fun with Keisha this weekend. They hadn't had a chance to hang out and have girl time since she had PJ so she was really looking forward to them getting to spend some quality time together. Paul would be busy with work; he had a few artists that were performing so that would keep him busy most of the time which was a good thing because she didn't want to be the third wheel. She also didn't want them to feel obligated to entertain her because they felt sorry for her.

By the time she made it to her hotel, the action on Bourbon Street was in full swing and it was only one in the afternoon. She checked into the Royal Sonesta and the receptionist was extremely pleasant. The hotel was gorgeous. She loved early American architecture and they had done a great job of preserving the French heritage of the area. The receptionist handed her a key fob and the tag said Presidential Suite.

"I'm sorry Miss but I had a reservation for the Bourbon Balcony Suite not the Presidential."

"Yes Ma'am I see that here but your room was upgraded as a courtesy."

When You Love Somebody

"By who."

"It doesn't say Ma'am but there is a note here with your name on it."

Cami took the note and opened it. She recognized Keisha's familiar chicken scratch immediately.

'Dear Sister-Cousin, I wanted to do something special for you and I knew if I told you about it you wouldn't have let me. I upgraded you to a room fit for a queen because that's what you are and have always been. Love you.'

Cami couldn't stop the tears that began to cascade down her face. She held the note close to her heart and smiled.

"Thank you" she said to the receptionist and grabbed her camera bag. The bell hop appeared and put the rest of her luggage on a cart. Matt had bought her the six piece purple Louis Vuitton luggage set from Paris. Whenever she used a piece of the set it reminded her of him but she loved the suitcases too much to get rid of them. The bell boy escorted her to the elevator and told

her to wave her key fob over the sensor. The
doors closed and the elevator went directly
to the fifth floor. She pressed the key fob
when she got in front of her room and the
double doors automatically opened. She
walked into what she thought was
someone's Park Avenue Apartment. There
was a seating area, a full dining room and a
huge piano in what she assumed was the
living room. She felt like little orphan Annie
when she first visited Daddy Warbucks'
mansion.

The bell boy brought her back to the present
when he asked, "Do you need anything else
Ma'am?"

"No, I'm fine. Thank you so much." Cami
smiled at him and fished around in her purse
until she found her wallet. She gave him a
twenty dollar bill and walked him to the
door."

"Thank you Ma'am enjoy your stay at the
Royal Sonesta."

"I will." Cami said half to him and half to
herself. The first thing she did was take her

When You Love Somebody

clothes off and run the shower. Airplanes always made her feel so dirty and the humidity in New Orleans made it hotter than Hades outside. She needed to hurry because she was supposed to be meeting Keisha at three for lunch. They were going to Emeril Lagasse's restaurant and she couldn't wait to see what they had on the menu. She had heard that their chicken and waffles were to die for so she definitely wanted to make sure she got a chance to taste it.

By the time she got to the restaurant it had to be at least 110 degrees. It didn't take much for her to sweat so just walking from the car to front of the restaurant had her dripping with perspiration. When she got to the hostess station, Keisha was standing there talking to someone but she couldn't see who it was so she motioned to the hostess to let Keisha know she was there. When she turned around, Cami realized that Keisha was talking to Matt. Really? She thought to herself. Keisha set her up? She was beginning to get upset until she saw the look on Matt's face when he realized she was standing behind Keisha and the way Keisha tried to use her body to shield her from Matt's view. Damn what a coincidence. She had managed to avoid him this entire time and it took her to travel halfway across the country to bump into him.

"Hi Cami how are you?"

"Hi Matt I'm good and you?"

"I've been better. "

Keisha interrupted the awkwardness of the moment to announce that she was going to let the hostess show her to their table. Matt and Cami just stood there looking at each other and then Matt blurted out, "You've put on some weight. It looks good and you have a glow around your face."

"Matt please that isn't a glow, its sweat. It's hot like fish grease down here."

"Nah, it's definitely more than sweat. Is there something you want to tell me?"

"Like what?"

When You Love Somebody

"Cami we have never lied to each other so please don't start now. Don't do this to me."

"Do what? I don't know what you're talking about."

"Okay since you don't want to just tell me. I'm going to ask you a question and I want you to look me in my eyes and tell me the honest to God truth."

"I have never lied to you Matt. I'm not a liar."

"I know you aren't. So please look me in my eyes."

Cami looked up at Matt and her hazel eyes were watery.

"Are you pregnant Camille?"

How could he tell? Cami asked herself. She was thrown so off guard that it took her a second to get her voice to make any sound.

"Answer my question Cami."

"I don't think so."

"What do you mean you don't think so? When was the last time you had your period?"

LatimaNicole

"I'm not doing this with you in the middle of a restaurant Matt."

"Answer my question Cami."

"About six weeks ago."

"So when were you going to tell me. I know you wasn't thinking about getting rid of my baby without telling me."

"Matt I don't even know if I am or not. My period could be late for a number of reasons, mainly stress. I haven't even taken a test yet let alone make a decision like that."

"So when do you plan on taking the test?"

"I'll worry about all of that when I get home. Right now I just want to enjoy New Orleans."

"Are you going to let me know what's up?"

"Yes you have a right to know either way but don't think that you are going to have any say so over what I choose to do with my body."

Matt rubbed his temples and yelled, "Fuck is you talking about Cami?"

"Lower your voice Matt."

When You Love Somebody

Keisha came running over and put her hand on Matt's shoulder. She had never heard him raise his voice even at Louise so she was a bit concerned. "Matt what's going on hunnie?"

He never took his eyes off of Cami or acknowledged Keisha.

"Cami, please do not play with me. I know things between us was fucked up but I'm asking you please don't do this."

"Do what Matt? You are jumping to conclusions for no reason."

"I have every reason I know what time it is you're the one in denial. Matter fact come on there's a Walgreen's up the block let's go."

Keisha stepped in the middle as Matt grabbed Cami's arm and tried to pull her out the door.

"Matt hold on what the hell is going on?"

"Keisha stay out of this. This is between me and Cami."

LatimaNicole

"Have you lost your fucking mind? If you don't let go of her arm, I'm gonna have the hostess call the police and lock your ass up." Matt reluctantly let Cami's arm go and said, "I'm sorry Cami. I'm bugging right now. I love you so much that it's driving me crazy. Can we go somewhere and talk?"

"There's nothing to talk about right now. I just want to get some food and hang out with Keish. I don't want to have to deal with us right now. Can you just be easy while we're down here and we'll talk when we get home?"

"Alright Cami, I'm gonna let you rock but trust me this ain't over."

Keisha looked at Matt and then looked at Cami. "What the hell did you say to him?"

"Nothing."

"Really Cami? You know you can't lie for shit so cut it out."

She didn't want to mention her possible pregnancy to Keisha or anybody else for that matter until she knew how she was going to handle the situation. "I'm serious. I didn't

When You Love Somebody

say anything to him. He's jumping to conclusions for no reason."

"So why was he trying to drag your ass to Walgreen's?"

"Because he done lost his damn mind now let's go eat. I don't have time for Matt's bullshit right now."

"Alright but I'm gonna tell you like Matt told you. This ain't over."

LatimaNicole

Epilogue

Fast forward nine months and Cami was in the Labor and Delivery suite at Long Island Jewish hospital. Who would have thought that her life would have changed so drastically in the last couple of years? She sure could never have imagined that she would be hours away from delivering her daughter. According to the Doctor Mari Bernice Cortlandt was minutes away from making her debut.

Matt was by her side telling her to breathe, Keisha and Paul were sitting on the couch with Mr. Cortlandt, Sonny, Maya and Misa. Everyone was waiting with baited breath for the princess to arrive. She looked over at Matt and squeezed his hand as the Doctor yelled for her to push. She took a deep breath and with all of her might she pushed her little angel into the world. Matt moved to the end of the bed and cut the umbilical cord and the baby began to cry.

When You Love Somebody

She could see Keisha out of the corner of her eye standing to the side crying.

It didn't seem real until Matt put the baby on her chest and bent down and kissed her on the forehead.

"Thank you Cami."

"Why are you thanking me?"

"Because although I love my kids and couldn't imagine my life without them, this baby was made from real love and I thank you for giving me a chance to know what that feels like."

"Matt you don't have to thank me. I feel the same way you feel."

"Then why won't you be my wife?"

"We've discussed this Matt. We need time to figure everything out. You know how I feel about marriage. It's forever, til death do us part. I'm not going to rush to marry you just because we have a baby. I need to know that we are going to ride this thing til the wheels fall off."

"Okay Cami. I'm not going to stop trying to make you my wife."

LatimaNicole

Their conversation was cut short by the kids barging from behind the curtain wanting to get a peek at their baby sister.

Misa was the least excited out of the three. She wasn't happy about not being the baby anymore but Sonny and Maya practically jumped in the bed with Cami and Mari. Matt had to restrain them so that the nurse could take the baby away to get cleaned.

"I'm gonna take these rascals downstairs to get something to eat. You want anything Cami?"

"No thank you I'm fine,"

"Okay we'll be back." "Pop you and Paul wanna take a walk with me and the kids?"

"Yeah youngblood. Let the ladies have some time together."

After they were gone, Keisha came and sat on the bed with Cami.

"I'm so proud of you sister-cousin. How are you feeling?"

"A little sore and a lot of tired but I'm okay."

When You Love Somebody

"I still can't believe you have a mini me. She looks just like you."

"I think she looks like her father. She just has my eyes and complexion."

"So how are things with you and Matt?"

"We're taking it day by day. He has been very supportive throughout my pregnancy. He made sure he was at every Doctor's appointment and he even decorated the guest room and turned it into a nursery. I haven't had to lift a finger the entire pregnancy."

"That's not what I meant. How are things with you and Matt?"

"I still love him and he still loves me but I'm just not ready to make that commitment yet. Even though he and his wife are separated they are still not divorced and you know what they say, 'the way you got him is the way you'll lose him'"

"Now you know that doesn't apply to Matt but I am curious why it's taking him so long to sign those papers."

LatimaNicole

"Girl I don't ask anymore. I guess you have to take the good, the bad and the ugly when you love somebody."

When You Love Somebody Book Club Discussion Questions

1. Was Cami and Matt's relationship based on real love or was it lust?

2. If you were Cam's friend, what type of advice would you give her regarding her relationship with Matt?

3. How did the parent-child dynamic affect the way the characters viewed their roles in relationships?

4. How does the absence of a father or father figure affect the way the women in the book deal with men?

5. Do agree with Cami's statement that Matt had no say so regarding what she chose to do with her body?

6. Do you believe that you get to choose who you fall in love with?

7. Would you consider Cami to be a home wrecker?

8. Would you have put up with Paul's cheating? If so how long?

9. Do you believe that marriage is forever?

10. Do you think that Cami will be bit by Karma?

When You Love Somebody

Contact

I would love to hear from you. You can reach out to me via social media.

Website – LatimaNicole.com

Facebook – LatimaNicole Author page

Instagram - @LatimaNicole1

Twitter - @LatimaNicole

Periscope - @LatimaNicole

www.ingramcontent.com/pod-product-compliance
Lightning Source LLC
Chambersburg PA
CBHW070059030726
47506CB00002B/523